'First of all,
what we did v

'But we're not goi
Soon we'll know if ~~you get~~ your sight back or
not. It won't make a difference to me. It might
make a difference to you. So can we put
things on hold until then? Please, Jonathan?'

He frowned, and she wondered what he was
thinking.

'If that's what you want, then of course that's
what we'll do. But let me say two things.
Whatever happens, whether I get my sight
back or not, I'll feel the same way about you,
Tania. I love you. And, if I do get my sight
back, then there's one thing I'm looking
forward to. The sight of you, waiting for me,
naked on my bed. It'll be the most wondrous
thing I've ever seen.'

It took all her strength. She wanted so much
to believe him.

Gill Sanderson, aka Roger Sanderson, started as a husband-and-wife team. At first Gill created the storyline, characters and background, asking Roger to help with the actual writing. But her job became more and more time-consuming and he took over all the work. He loves it!

Roger has written many Medical Romance™ books for Harlequin Mills & Boon®. Ideas come from three of his children—Helen is a midwife, Adam a health visitor, Mark a consultant oncologist. Weekdays are for work; weekends find Roger walking in the Lake District or Wales.

Recent titles by the same author:

THE NURSE'S DILEMMA
A FULL RECOVERY
MALE MIDWIFE
MARRIAGE AND MATERNITY

THE CONSULTANT'S RECOVERY

BY

GILL SANDERSON

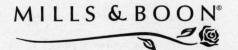

MILLS & BOON®

First published in Great Britain 2002
Harlequin Mills & Boon Limited,
Eton House, 18-24 Paradise Road, Richmond, Surrey TW9 1SR

© Gill Sanderson 2002

ISBN 0 263 83068 3

Set in Times Roman 10½ on 12 pt.
03-0502-49780

Printed and bound in Spain
by Litografia Rosés, S.A., Barcelona

PROLOGUE

DR JONATHAN KNIGHT had come back onto his ward a day early, and he wasn't a happy man when he arrived. He looked thoughtfully at the blue-overalled electrician in front of him. 'We were assured all this work would be finished in three days,' he said gently, 'I gather you've been here for five.'

The man scrambled to his feet and tried unsuccessfully to hide the mug of tea he was clutching. 'I came across a few problems,' he offered. 'You can't always tell what you'll find when—'

Jonathan rode over his story. 'I'm sure you can cope,' he said. 'Your firm said that you were an excellent workman. Now, I take it you will be finished by…shall we say the end of the day?'

His voice was soft, in no way threatening. But suddenly the electrician decided that, yes, it would be a good idea to finish by the end of the day. 'I'll work through my dinner-break,' he mumbled.

Jonathan smiled. 'No need for that. As I said, I'm sure you'll cope.'

He stood there watching as the workman gathered his tools and moved quickly out of the little anteroom where he had been so comfortable. Then Jonathan shrugged. If all his problems were so easy to solve as this!

He walked down the corridor to the nurses' station. He could hear the mutter of voices, the clatter of nurses' feet, a clang from the sluice. He could smell the all-pervasive hospital smell, not unpleasant but strangely comforting. For the past five days he had been at a conference held at a country house in Cambridgeshire. He had enjoyed the course—had enjoyed meeting colleagues and had learned quite a lot. But now he was home and it was good to be back.

'Jonathan…er, Dr Knight…I didn't know you were back!'

Jonathan smiled down at Staff Nurse Amy Parkin, a small rounded lady aged about fifty.

'Jonathan will be fine, as usual,' he said. 'I came back a little early and I dropped in to see Eleanor if she's around. Everything been all right, Amy?'

Amy sniffed. 'Apart from the electrician.' She glanced as the man trotted down the corridor towards them, carrying a stepladder over his shoulder. 'He seems to have two speeds—dead slow and stop.'

'I've had a word with him and we'll review the situation this evening. And who's this?' Behind Amy was a nervous-looking girl in the dark uniform of a probationer nurse.

'This is Jenny Lee,' said Amy. 'She'll be with us for a few weeks.'

Jonathan took Jenny's hand and shook it gently. 'Pleased to meet you, Jenny. I hope you enjoy your stay with us. Any problems, any questions, ask Staff here, or me or any of the others. You learn by asking questions.'

'Yes, Doctor, thank you, Doctor,' Jenny managed. She was obviously having difficulty coping with this courtesy. But Jonathan always made a point of knowing his nurses, of being aware of their characters, their careers, their hopes.

'I gather you were in Orthopedics before. You'll find that infectious diseases is different, but you'll learn.'

'Jonathan! Why didn't you tell me you were here? We weren't expecting you till tomorrow.'

Jonathan turned to meet a smiling man with wild red hair and a crumpled shirt and tie. Only his stethoscope and white coat showed that he was a doctor. It was Joe Simms, his junior registrar and a very good friend.

'Joe! I guess I just couldn't keep away.' Jonathan grinned at his friend, then he frowned slightly. 'In fact, I came in to have a quick word with Eleanor. You haven't seen her, have you?'

'She's got a meeting with one of the Chief Executive's money men, but when she hears you're here she'll be up like a shot. Shall I phone down to say you're asking for her?'

'I'd like that, but it's not important really. I just want— Excuse me a minute, Joe.'

He had been vaguely aware of someone else in the corridor, hesitating then trying to slide past the little chatting group without attracting any attention. Jonathan looked at the man—a youth really—and he remembered him.

He was thin, pale-faced. He had studs in one eyebrow, his lip and his nose. And he didn't look happy at being spotted. 'Just...just going to see my mate,' he muttered. Then, from somewhere, he gained strength. 'It's visiting time, and it's a free country. You can't stop me.'

Jonathan stared at the lad. 'I spoke to you a week ago. I told you that you weren't welcome on my ward.'

'Yes, well, Dane phoned me and said he wasn't feeling so good. I thought I'd come in and—'

'You've brought him something? A little present for

Dane from his mates outside? You'd heard that I'd be away till tomorrow?'

'No! I haven't brought in nothing! Honestly, mister, I…' It was obvious to everyone there that he was lying.

Jonathan strode across the corridor, stood close to the youth so that he was effectively pinned against the wall. 'Which pocket is it in?'

'Here, you can't threaten me. I'll go if you want but…'

Jonathan leaned against the corridor wall, one arm on each side of the youth's head. 'Tell me which pocket or we stand here till Security come for you. And they'll send for the police, I promise. Which pocket?' The last two words were very quiet—and yet the threat was obvious.

'Inside pocket.' The muffled words were barely audible.

Jonathan thrust his hand in the inside pocket and took out a small paper packet. He tore it open, sniffed the contents. 'Because of stuff like this,' he said, now speaking very slowly and clearly, 'your friend will probably die. This drug might make him happier for a few minutes, but it would do no good for his long-term prospects. Now get out. If you come back, and especially if I catch you passing on this stuff, I'll have you arrested for dealing. Understand?'

The youth looked at him sullenly. Jonathan whispered, 'I said, do you understand?'

'Yes, mister.'

'Have you a card, Joe?' Jonathan kept one hand on the youth's shoulder as he turned to speak to his junior registrar. Joe took a card from his briefcase and handed it to Jonathan, who gave it to the youth. 'Keep this. It's the address of a charity that tries to help addicts

like you. If you ask, they'll try to help you. It's entirely
up to you. I don't want to see you here on my ward as
a patient, but if you carry on as you're doing, then I
suspect I will. Do you really want to finish like Dane?
Now, off you go!'

The youth looked wide-eyed at the group, then scuttled off down the corridor.

Jonathan rejoined the group. 'Good to have you
back, practising medicine in a discreet and gentle way,'
said Joe. 'You know, that lad had rights—of a sort—
which you interfered with.'

'No drug dealer has rights on my ward,' Jonathan
said. 'Let's hope he realises that now.'

He took the packet he was holding into the sluice
room and they heard him flush it away. Then he
washed his hands. When he rejoined the group, he said
conversationally to Jenny, 'This is an infectious diseases ward, Jenny. Unfortunately, various diseases—or
illnesses—are the result of drug abuse. Hepatitis, HIV
and so on. Perhaps we shouldn't have these patients on
this ward—combating drug addiction is a specialised
branch of medicine itself. But we do get ill drug addicts. Many of them persist in trying to take drugs, in
spite of what we can prescribe them—methadone usually. And I won't have it.'

'Perhaps you'd like a cup of coffee now?' Staff
Nurse Parkin said. 'Now that everyone knows that
you're back.'

To her evident surprise Jenny was invited to walk
round the ward with Amy, Joe and Jonathan. 'Not a
proper ward round,' Jonathan explained. 'I'd just like
to remind myself of things.'

Eventually they went into a side ward holding just
one person. As ever, when he saw someone on his ward

suffering because of self-inflicted damage, Jonathan felt great pity. Why did people do things like this to themselves?

'This is Dane Bland,' Jonathan said gently to Jenny. 'It looks like he's not feeling too well today.'

They looked at the emaciated figure lying in the bed. He tried to lift his head from the pillow, but it took too much effort. He was a young man—a boy even—perhaps aged nineteen, but the wasted face, protruding jawbone and cheek-bones made him look much older.

'I'll be all right soon, Dr Knight,' Dane managed to mutter. 'Just a bit off today.'

'You're making some progress, but not as much as I'd like. Dane, you can't carry on taking drugs. I talked to your mate this morning, took his stash off him. He won't be in to see you again.'

'Tony! But he said you—'

'Apparently you asked to use the portable phone,' Jonathan said. 'You're supposed to use it to keep in touch with your family, not to order drugs.'

Dane was too exhausted to argue. 'Whatever you say,' he said. Jonathan looked at him a few moments longer, then they all silently left the room.

'How d'you feel about patients who harm themselves, Jenny?' he asked when they were some distance down the corridor.

She thought a moment. 'I've just been in Orthopedics,' she said. 'We get a lot of young lads who had crashed motorbikes. They break arms, legs, any bone you can mention. And then they find that just sitting, waiting for the bone to heal, is terrible. They're lads, they have to be up and moving. So they move and they often slow down the healing.'

'And what can you do about it?'

'Not a lot. Explain, wait and watch. But it gets very irritating when they put their progress back a month by sheer stupidity.'

'You've got the right idea, Jenny.' Jonathan thought that the young probationer would fit in on his ward.

As they walked back to the nurses' station Jonathan saw the flash of long blonde hair and a brightly coloured dress turning into the doctors' room. 'You got through to Eleanor, then?' he asked Joe.

'She said she'd be right up. Said that you should have let her know that you were back.' Jonathan saw that Joe was being deliberately noncommittal.

'There's work to do on the ward,' Joe went on. 'I'll leave you two alone in the doctors' room for the next half-hour. She can bring you up to date with what's been going on.'

Is it that obvious? Jonathan thought bleakly to himself. He wasn't looking forward to this conversation.

Amy also announced that she had plenty to do, that she would just send in Jenny with a pot of coffee. 'Thanks,' said Jonathan. He pushed open the door to the doctors' room.

It was a small room, windowless, with a noticeboard full of disregarded pieces of paper, a narrow bed in one corner where overnight staff might catch a couple of hours' sleep, desks, a set of easy chairs and coffee-tables. Jonathan had had some happy moments in this room—and some not so happy.

'Hello, Eleanor,' he said flatly.

He stood passively as she ran to him, enveloped him in a hug and tried to kiss his lips. This he avoided by putting his arms round her, leaning over her shoulder.

Eleanor—Dr Eleanor Page, Jonathan's specialist registrar—was a beauty. Everyone said so. Eleanor knew this, and accepted people's homage as her right. Perhaps because of this, Jonathan thought, she didn't like it when she didn't get her own way.

She was tall, with long blonde hair and a figure that was full without being too opulent. Her make-up was expert and immaculate—always. She dressed with care. Even if it was an emergency there were no suddenly thrown-on garments for Eleanor.

'Why didn't you tell me you were coming back early? I could have met you, we could have... There's all sorts of things we could have done.'

'All sorts of things,' he repeated. He tried gently to ease her away but Eleanor wasn't going to be moved.

'I'm not letting go till you've kissed me properly.' She pouted. 'Show me that you're pleased to see me.'

'Yes, you will let go. That new nurse is bringing us some coffee. And you know I'm always pleased to see my SR.'

Eleanor released him. She had a keen sense of propriety and felt that nurses and other ancillary staff shouldn't know about the intimate affairs of doctors. 'Aren't you pleased to see me—Eleanor—not just the woman you work with?'

Again Jonathan sighed. He felt he didn't deserve this. He'd tried to be fair. 'Sit down, Eleanor. There's things we have to talk about, things we have to settle.'

'Of course there are. After that last board meeting, when you drove me home, I knew that—'

There was a timid tap on the door and in came Jenny, carrying a tray with coffee and biscuits. Jonathan was glad of the interruption. He smiled at Jenny and thanked her, then took the tray and sat down with it. There was nothing Eleanor could do but sit down, too. She watched, irritated, as Jonathan poured the coffee from the pot.

Now they were sitting in the easy chairs, facing each other across the coffee-table, each with a cup in hand.

'After I drove you home from the board meeting,' he went on, 'you knew what?'

'I knew that things were the same between us as they'd been before. The way you kissed me, Jonathan. That wasn't the kiss of someone who didn't care.'

'I kissed you because you're a very attractive woman, we'd had a pleasant evening and you obviously wanted to be kissed! If anything, you kissed me!'

'Not a very gentlemanly thing to say,' said Eleanor, 'but I'll forgive you. Now, you got my letter saying I'd booked a weekend up in Kendal?'

Jonathan reached in his inside pocket and drew out a pink envelope. He passed it over. 'I got your letter. Eleanor, this is the time for straight speaking. Five years ago we were lovers. It was good while it lasted, but it ended and I like to think we stayed friends, though we didn't see much of each other. Then I got the consultancy here. And a year ago you applied to be my specialist reg. I didn't think it a good idea, but you persuaded me it would be wrong of me to stand in the way of your career. So you got the job.'

'I'm a good registrar,' Eleanor said sullenly. 'You've said I am.'

'You're an excellent registrar. But our love affair is done, it's over. I will not go with you to Kendal. We're friends and nothing more.'

'Jonathan!' She crashed down her cup and stood, her blue eyes wide with incredulity. 'You can't mean that! I remember the way you kissed me! That wasn't the kiss of a friend.'

'It was. Eleanor, all there is between us now is friendship.'

Now her eyes filled with tears but he didn't relent. He remembered from their past how easily Eleanor had been able to cry.

'Can't we just wait a while?' she whispered. 'There's no need to decide anything now. Let's see how we feel in, say, another three or four—'

'No, Eleanor! Whatever we had is dead! Now, I've had enough of this conversation. I've got work to do and so have you. Let's do it!'

From long and bitter experience he knew this was the only way to deal with Eleanor when she was in this mood. She could cling like a limpet.

He stood, opened the door for her as she swept out. Then he followed her down the corridor. It had been bad—but it could have been worse.

They came to the swing door entrance to the ward together. Jonathan pulled open the door again, indicating that she should go first. Outside on the landing was the electrician, balanced on the top of his stepladder, holding a heavy electric drill.

The electrician glanced downwards as they came out. He lost his balance, the stepladder started to wobble. Then it crashed downwards—straight towards Eleanor.

Jonathan didn't have time to think. He leapt forward, his shoulder hitting the small of Eleanor's back, throwing her forward into an undignified heap.

And then there was blackness.

He was told afterwards what happened then. There was a shout and the crash of the stepladder bouncing off the floor. A moment's silence, and then the workman's anxious voice. 'Hey, mate, are you all right?'

And then he went on, with increasing panic, 'Doctor! *Doctor!*'

When Eleanor managed to roll over, to try to work out what had happened, Jonathan was lying face downwards, perfectly still, the stepladder across his back. A nervous electrician looked down at him. And the heavy drill lay across the back of Jonathan's head. Blood seeped steadily from under it.

A second later Joe and Amy rushed through the door. Joe threw the drill aside, then tried to stem the sudden rush of blood with a cloth. 'I'll fetch a sterile pack,' Amy said, 'and I'll send for a trolley.'

When she returned, Joe was taking Jonathan's pulse and at the same time trying to work out exactly where the drill had landed. 'We're going to need a hard collar as well, Staff,' he muttered. 'I think it missed his neck but it could have damaged the brain stem. I want a neurologist to see him as quickly as possible.

'There's Charles Forsythe on the ground floor. I know he does a round this morning. Shall I bleep him?'

'No. Phone the ward first, get someone to tell him in person. He's a pal of Jonathan's he'll be here like a shot.'

Amy looked up. 'Eleanor? Are you hurt at all?'

'No. Just a bit bruised. Staff, he pushed me out of the way and got hit himself. If he hadn't, I—'

'Go and sit down,' Amy said gently. 'Get the nurse to make you some tea. I think you're in shock.'

She saw Joe's fingers feeling gently round the back of Jonathan's skull, trying to discover if there was a fracture. A rattling suggested that someone had brought a trolley, but Joe didn't want Jonathan moved just yet. And then, further down the corridor, she heard the lift doors sigh open and another, confidence-inspiring voice said, 'Do we have a problem here?'

An older man knelt by her and felt Jonathan's skull as Joe gave a quick report. 'We can move him,' he said eventually. 'I want him down on my ward now. I've got a bed he can use. If you want, you can come with me, Joe.'

'I want,' said Joe. And all the time Jonathan Knight lay motionless.

Jonathan felt terrible. He didn't know why. He wasn't really sure who or where he was, all he knew was that he had a headache worse than any pain he had ever suffered in his life before. He must have been unconscious but now he was coming to. He didn't want to come to. He'd rather go back to sleep. He wanted to sink back into the nothingness he was coming out of. Being awake hurt.

Why *was* he here? He was Dr Jonathan Knight, he was a consultant, he'd been looking round his ward and...and nothing. He remembered talking to Joe, to Amy, to Eleanor...and then nothing.

'How d'you feel, Jonathan? You must have a headache but...otherwise how d'you feel?'

A voice, a voice he recognised. It was his friend Charles Forsythe. What was he doing here? And where was here? And why was he being kept in the dark?

'Charles? What's going on? What is this place and can you, please, put on the light?'

'You had a slight accident. One of those heavy drills fell on your head. Now, keep quite still.' He sensed someone leaning over him, for a moment caught the smell of an expensive shaving lotion, felt breath on his face. Someone was very close to him. Charles's voice asked, 'Can you see anything, Jonathan?'

'Not a thing. I—' Suddenly even the throbbing pain in his head was forgotten. He was a doctor, things were making sense to him. He reached up, caught Charles's hand in his. He could feel that Charles was holding a slim metal tube and he knew what it was. A torch. And he hadn't seen a thing.

Terror rushed through his body. He tried to jerk upright, but Charles caught his shoulders and eased him back on the bed. 'You've got to relax, Jonathan, just take it easy. I'm examining you. You've had a very nasty knock.'

'I don't remember anything!'

'Retrospective amnesia. A bang on the head often causes you to forget things. Don't let it worry you.'

'That's not worrying me. Charles, I can't see a thing. I'm not a fool. I'm blind, aren't I?'

Charles's silence told him all he needed to know.

CHAPTER ONE

IT WAS hot, really hot, the kind of summer that came only occasionally in England. There was no sign of it changing either. The weather forecasters were saying that this could last through July and well into August.

Tania Richardson walked across the lawns of the Frederick Bramley School for the Blind, smiling at the young people who were sitting outside, making the most of the good weather. Making the most appeared to mean wearing as little as possible. Not like herself. Even in the hottest weather Tania preferred to be well covered. She hoped there wouldn't be too many cases of sunburn. There would certainly be a few.

She passed the open-air swimming pool, nodded at the guard on his high chair, saw the students swimming alone—a confidence-building exercise. And in this weather, a welcome one.

She entered the administration block, went to the door marked DERRICK GEE, MANAGER. Outside she stopped and sighed. She loved her job as a rehabilitation worker, but having to work for Derrick wasn't one of the things she liked best about it. She waved at the secretary and entered.

'Come in, Tania, come in. Sit down. Let me get you a glass of iced orange. It's good to see you.'

Derrick was always pleasant, always polite. Perhaps too polite. Tania had a feeling that sooner or later he was going to want to take their friendship a stage further. And that she didn't want.

Derrick was in his late thirties, about ten years older than her. He was tall, thin, balding and tended to wear super-fashionable clothes that just didn't suit him. The baggy linen suit he was wearing now must have cost a fortune, but it did nothing for him. Tania sighed again.

She sat, accepted the iced orange and was glad when to begin with Derrick was businesslike. 'As you know, you're here on a temporary contract, Tania. This can be terminated by either side at a week's notice. I don't like this, I want you to have job security. We've applied for funding for another full-time rehabilitation worker. When it comes through I want you to apply, and I know you'll get the job.'

She hadn't expected this so soon. Cautiously, she said, 'that's very nice of you, Derrick. But I'm quite happy working the way I am at present.'

'But don't you want the security of a permanent position?' He was surprised at her lack of enthusiasm.

'Well, yes. But there are reasons—family reasons— why this job suits me the way it is. I'm sorry, I can't really explain.'

This was a bit of a lie, but there was no way she would explain to Derrick just why she didn't want to be tied to a job. Two years ago she had been betrayed by a man, nastily, viciously. For three months she had thought that he had been the man of her dreams, the man she would spend the rest of her life with. When she had told him—showed him even—what worried her, he had talked about her, laughed at her. Then he'd laughed even more when she'd found out that she had to carry on working for him. No way would she give any man that kind of power over her again. She didn't want a permanent job.

Derrick looked upset. 'That's a pity. I thought you'd be pleased at this offer. I thought we might celebrate somehow.'

'Perhaps,' she said, 'perhaps some time. But at the moment I've rather a lot to do.'

'Of course.' Derrick was disappointed but he wasn't going to show it. 'Incidentally, I came to work very early this morning. You were swimming. It looked wonderful—I thought I might join you tomorrow morning.'

She was cautious. 'I don't swim every morning.'

'Perhaps not.' Obviously Derrick felt that nothing was going right for him today. Time to be businesslike.

As he leafed through the papers on his desk Tania sighed again. She'd thought she'd be undisturbed, swimming in the early morning. But Derrick had seen her—and she knew he'd turn up the next morning. Too bad for him, she wouldn't be there. Too bad for her as well, she'd enjoyed her early morning swims.

'I've got a new client for you,' Derrick said eventually. 'I assessed him myself in hospital yesterday. We also have reports here from the psychologist, the social worker and the neurologist.'

'Neurologist?' This was unusual but not unheard of. Usually there was a report from the consultant optometrist.

'Yes, the neurologist. There's nothing whatsoever wrong with this man's eyes. He had a massive blow to the back of the head which damaged the optic nerve and the visual cortex.'

'I see.' Most of the cases that were referred to them were as a result of disease or damage to the eye itself. But it was a medical truism—all seeing was done in the brain. Trauma to the brain could make a man blind even though his eyes functioned perfectly.

'This is a bit of an unusual case,' Derrick went on. 'We have to do the best for this man. He's a hospital consultant and a close personal friend of the neurologist.'

'I do my best for all of my clients,' Tania said, 'no matter who their friends are or who they are.' Derrick's remark had irritated her.

'I'm sure you do.' Now that Derrick had got the message, he decided to get rid of Tania as quickly as possible.

'The man's name is Jonathan Knight. He's a consultant in infectious diseases, aged thirty-five, not married and apparently no family available. But there's no shortage of friends, and no shortage of money. An independent sort of chap. At the moment he's completely blind but there's just a chance that he might get his sight back if he has an operation. The neurologist still has to give it the go-ahead. But he's not going just to sit and wait and see what might happen. He wants to proceed as if he's going to be blind all his life.'

'There are worse ways of dealing with things,' Tania said. 'I like a fighter.'

Derrick pushed the file over to her. 'Go and see him when you can,' he said, and then made one last despairing attempt. 'You say you're busy tonight?'

'Very busy,' Tania said.

'My name's Joe Simms,' the friendly voice on the phone said. 'I work with Jonathan and I'm a friend as well. Are you the professional help that's been promised us?'

'I'm a rehabilitation worker, yes. My name's Tania

Richardson. When would it be convenient for me to come to see Mr Knight? Or is it Dr Knight?'

'He likes Dr Knight, he's not a surgeon. You can come at any time—the sooner the better. Can you come now?'

She thought of the address. 'I'll be there in twenty minutes.'

Dr Knight lived in some style. She drove to a luxurious block of flats overlooking the river. She had to park outside—you needed a card to open the gates that led to the garages below the flats. When she walked to the entrance she saw that on the other side of the flats there was a large walled garden, with walks, well-tended flower-beds, garden furniture. A few residents were sitting there. It looked very pleasant. That would be handy later.

She rang the bell marked 'Knight', aware that she was being observed by a camera high in the wall above. That didn't worry her—there were security cameras all over the Frederick Bramley School. Some evil people thought that a blind school would provide easy pickings.

A voice spoke to her out of a grille. 'Miss Richardson? I'm opening the door. Take the lift to the top floor.'

She entered a luxurious lobby, then a wood-panelled lift that whisked her silently upwards. There was only one flat on the top floor, the penthouse. And on the landing, waiting for her, was a tall, engaging man about her own age, with a shock of red hair.

'Hi, I'm Joe Simms. I'm Jonathan's junior registrar—just a general dogsbody. I make life on the ward easier for him.' She took to Joe at once.

'How d'you like this bit of your work, then?'

He pulled a face. 'I hate it, I feel so helpless. I'm looking forward to you telling me what can be done. Incidentally, Miss Richardson, perhaps I should warn you. He used to be calm, but recently he seems to have developed a temper.'

'At the moment he's entitled to one,' she said. 'It's not an unusual reaction to sudden blindness.'

Joe led her into the flat, and she caught her breath as they walked into the living room. All of the far wall was a giant triangular window. Through it she could see the river, with ships sailing up the channel to the sea beyond.

It was an austere room, obviously a man's room. The floor was polished wood, with a deep red Persian rug. Furniture was minimal and there was hardly anything on the plain walls. It was the room of a man who knew exactly what he wanted.

Then she saw him. He was sitting in a rocking chair by the window. At first she couldn't make out much about him because of the light that shone round him, and for a moment she wondered if he'd sat there on purpose.

Joe said, 'Jonathan, this is Miss Richardson, your rehabilitation worker.'

'Rehabilitation? It makes me sound like a criminal.' He stood. 'It would be wrong to say that I'm pleased to see you, Miss Richardson, wouldn't it? I can't see you and I'm not very pleased.'

She walked towards him. 'Let's shake hands anyway,' she said. 'Boxers do it before they fight, don't they?'

He laughed as she reached for his hand. She was surprised at how gently he held it. 'I hope we don't have to fight,' he said.

First, there was his voice. It was deep—confident usually, she thought, but now sounding a little harsh. She was closer now and could see him more clearly. It was still hot and he was dressed casually in khaki chinos and a white T-shirt. She was aware of his body, the muscles of his arms, chest, shoulders. He was lightly suntanned, but through being outdoors rather than lying in a salon.

She could read body language. This was a man who normally would dominate a room, just by being in it. He had the voice, the body, and normally he would have the confidence. But now there was something about the angle of his head, the way he hunched his shoulders, that suggested he was unsure of himself. And he hated it.

Then she saw his face. His dark hair was longer than usual, as if he cared nothing for fashion. It wasn't a good-looking face but a tough one. There were deep frown lines on his head and round his eyes. He would never be a relaxed man—and now he was less relaxed than ever. Tania felt an unfamiliar tightening in her throat. This man was going to be a challenge! But what sort of challenge?

Newly blinded adults reacted in a variety of ways. There was anything from calm acceptance to abject terror. She suspected that this man's reaction would surprise her. He would be different from any case she'd dealt with before.

She had to make the right impression at once. 'I'm pleased to meet you, Dr Knight,' she said. 'I'm hoping we can work well together.'

'Work well? Aren't you here to help me?'

'Certainly not. I'm here to make sure you can help yourself.'

Then he smiled and his face was transfigured. Before he had been frightening. Now he was friendship itself.

'That's an answer that I like,' he said. 'Joe, you ought to be getting back to the ward. Phone me this evening, I want to know how young Dane is getting on. We may need to up his dosage. And any problem, don't forget I'm here. I can still advise.'

Nerving herself, Tania interrupted. 'Dr Knight, I'm pleased to see you taking an interest in things, but right now you have other priorities.'

He scowled. 'Let's get this straight Miss Richardson. In ten day's time a locum consultant will be taking over my job. Until that time I'm in charge. I've got a good staff, and I've every faith in them. But until the locum comes, I'm responsible.'

'There are things that I've got to make clear, too,' she said. 'You've had a very nasty physical—and emotional—experience. Blindness is emotionally traumatic, it can affect people in different ways. If you're a good doctor you should know that your medical judgement could be suspect.'

'What! Are you telling me my job?'

Until that time she'd never realised just how threatening a soft voice could be, but she managed to keep the quaver out of her own voice. 'I wouldn't dream of telling you your job. But I'm referring to my own, quite extensive experience.'

'I see.' For a moment there was a silence. 'Joe, if I suggest something that really worries you, you have my permission to refer to anyone else you think experienced.'

'I would anyway,' Joe said laconically. 'I think Miss Richardson has a valid point, though I suspect it's not true in your case. See you later, Jonathan. Bye, Miss Richardson.' And he was gone.

'Alone at last,' Jonathan said as the door closed.

'I suspect you're more alone than you've ever been in your life before,' she replied.

'You could say that. But I'll cope.'

'I'm sure you will.' For some reason she was finding it harder to deal with this man than any other client she had ever had before. There was a hardness to him that she couldn't penetrate.

'Would you like me to make you a cup of tea or coffee?' she asked.

'No. I'll make us both a hot drink. I've spent the morning arranging things so I can do that small thing. Amazing how such a simple skill becomes difficult when you can't see where you've hidden the tea caddy.'

'You make the tea but I want to watch,' she said. 'Perhaps I can suggest a couple of things. Then we can talk. Incidentally, are you going to be on your own tonight? Are you happy about that?'

'I'll be on my own because that's what I want. Joe offered to stay, so did…someone else, but I want to be on my own. Why?'

Tania noticed the reference to someone else, but decided not to pry. 'Well…family or friends are usually very useful in the first few days,' she said carefully. 'Both to do practical things and—'

'And to act as an emotional crutch? That I do *not* need. Joe will call every day but I don't want anyone at night. Isn't that what you people want? For us to be self-sufficient?'

'Ultimately, yes. But friends or family can ease the transition. This reaction of yours—that you're going to look after yourself no matter what. You might think it shows independence. But it might not. It might show fear masquerading as bravado.'

'You're saying I'm afraid!' There was that frightening voice again.

She tried not to show him that she was afraid—of him. 'An instant change from complete sight to total blindness? You'd be a fool not to be afraid, Dr Knight. I know I would be.'

'Calling a patient afraid and a fool. Remind me never to employ you as a doctor, Miss Richardson. Your bedside manner is alarming.'

But Tania thought there was a grudging acceptance of her.

They were now in the kitchen, as neat and spartan as the living room, she noted. She watched as he slid his hand along the back wall of the polished steel counter, felt for the kettle and filled it, using a finger to determine when it was full enough.

'Tea or coffee, Miss Richardson? Until I get more skilled I'm afraid it can only be instant coffee.'

'I'd prefer tea, please. Milk but no sugar.'

There were mugs neatly arranged at the back of the counter, a box of teabags and differently shaped boxes of coffee and sugar. Jonathan turned and groped inside an enormous fridge for a carton of milk. She let him get on with it. He was clumsy, unskilled, but he was trying, and she had never met anyone who did so well without professional tuition. She noticed that the most difficult thing for him to do was to pour out the boiling water. He managed by not filling the mugs.

'You've done very well but I'll carry these into the living room,' she said finally. 'Don't expect to be expert at once.'

She followed him as he found his way back to the living room by trailing his fingers along the wall. He made his way back to the rocking chair, then turned towards her. 'I'd fetch you a chair,' he said, 'but—'

'I can carry my own chair, thank you. And I'll put our mugs on this coffee-table between us.'

And then they were sitting facing each other.

'The first two things we usually teach are trailing—that's using your fingers to navigate—and making a cup of tea,' she said. 'You seem to have done both yourself. You even find your way back to your favorite chair.'

'I usually sit in this chair when I come home,' he said. 'I have a cup of coffee and I...I use my telescope to look at the passing ships or the Welsh hills.' He nodded towards a corner. There she saw a large brass telescope, now neatly folded away. 'On a good clear day you can see right over to Snowdonia.'

'Well, you can't see much now, it's too misty.' She didn't want him to think about what he couldn't do. She also thought she could see lines of fatigue in his face, but knew she would never get him to admit to being tired. For a while they would just chat gently.

'I love your flat. It's so definitely masculine—this could never be a woman's room.'

'I grew up in women's rooms,' he said enigmatically, 'so now I don't have a single knick-knack. Apart from my Diana, that is.'

'Diana?'

'A little bronze—it's over on the bookshelf behind you. Go and have a look if you like.'

She did. There was the bronze—a sculpture of a naked goddess running with her dogs. She was glorious, the essence of female beauty.

'Why is she so shiny?' Tania asked. 'Do you polish her?'

'No. I hold her. Sometimes I think I can feel her beauty through my hands.' Then he obviously decided he had given away too much.

'Let's be practical,' he said. 'Come and tell me what I can expect.'

Tania returned to her seat. 'I gather there's a chance you might regain your sight.'

'A chance, no more. Charles Forsythe, the neurologist, is a friend of mine. He say's it's possible. I asked him what the odds were but he wouldn't say.' Jonathan grinned. 'These doctors are very hard to pin down, aren't they? But perhaps the chances are fifty-fifty, or sixty-forty, or even seventy-thirty?'

'In whose favour?'

'No one can tell. But I've decided to act as if my sight has gone permanently. That way I can't be disappointed.'

'An interesting reaction,' she said carefully. 'I think you're probably very wise.'

'Tell me how people normally cope. I want to know what's normal.'

'There is no normal. Coping is as various as people are. But, remember, it's no sign of weakness to accept worry, fear and so on. If you accept those as normal, you'll come through them faster.'

'I see. But if I feel fear, Miss Richardson, I want to keep it to myself.'

She sighed. 'Losing your sight is like losing a friend or relation. It's like a bereavement. There are stages you have to go through before you come to full acceptance, stages like horror and anger and even guilt and self-reproach. A lot of people just feel numb—there's nothing they can do. And it's almost impossible to avoid this process.'

'So that's what I have to look forward to?'

'You are a human being, Dr Knight.'

He thought for a moment. 'Not much of a prospect, is it?' he asked with a grin, and she found herself smiling back. When he smiled he was a different person.

'Let's go through the practical arrangements for the next few days,' she said. 'And I'd like to check heating and so on. Are there any fires or anything like that? Could you burn yourself?'

In fact, there was little she had to do. Having money certainly made things easier. Every morning he had a lady come in to clean and do his washing and ironing. She had offered to stay a further hour so she would cook a breakfast, make sandwiches or something for later. Friends would certainly drop in—Joe had said he would be there every day. If he wanted, he could order take-away meals on the phone—there was a very good service close by and he already had an account there.

'You've worked out how to use the phone. I want you to memorise one more number,' she said. 'This is a helpline—any time, day or night, you're in trouble, call.'

'That'll be handy to know,' he said seriously. 'Now, when will you be coming back?'

She thought of her schedule—she could reorganise a few things and… 'Tomorrow afternoon?' she asked.

'Looking forward to it. You can teach me how to cook.' Then he paused and said, 'Looking forward isn't the right phrase, is it?'

Tania thought for a moment that his guard had slipped, that he had revealed something of the pain he must feel. It made him so much more human. 'Looking forward will do fine,' she said. 'Incidentally—if you want—my name is Tania.'

'A good name. And I'm Jonathan. But I don't answer to John or Johnny.'

It was time for her to go. She had done all that was possible in a first visit. She stood and turned her head, and as she did so he reached out his hand to shake hers. His hand touched her breast, was instantly withdrawn.

'Sorry,' he said.

'Don't worry, it happens all the time.' Then she shook his hand and left.

It had only been the gentlest of touches—as she'd said, the kind of accident that happened all the time. But she thought she could still feel where he had touched her. Why was her pulse racing? Why was this man affecting her so much?

CHAPTER TWO

TANIA'S first visit the next day was very different.

Ronnie Slack was forty, and he had diabetic retinopathy. Some twenty years ago he had become diabetic, and then, one of the sad possibilities of the disease, tiny blood vessels had started to leak in his retinas. In spite of laser treatment, Ronnie's sight had deteriorated, eventually he'd haemorrhaged and a year ago he'd become completely blind. Some people would have regarded this as a challenge, and met it as best they could. Ronnie had just given way.

He was sitting, half-undressed, on his dirty settee. Loud pop music blared out from his radio—Ronnie spent hours listening to Radio One. Behind him she could see the kitchen, carefully planned and installed to be blind-person friendly. She had spent hours—days—trying to show Ronnie how to use it. Now the sink was piled high with dirty dishes, probably from the last four or five meals.

'You haven't washed up, Ronnie,' she said. She tried to keep her tone light. It wasn't her place to judge.

'Didn't feel like it. I don't feel too good, Tania. D'you mind doing it yourself?'

She ignored this suggestion. 'We had your GP out to see you last week. He said you were fine, but that you needed more exercise and possibly less food.'

'Eating is the only real pleasure I get these days,' Ronnie said glumly. 'You wouldn't want to stop that, would you?'

A surprising number of her clients never did feel sorry for themselves. Ronnie wasn't one of them. Again she reminded herself that it wasn't her place to judge. She could only imagine what being blind must be like.

'Let's start with the washing-up, shall we?' she said. 'You do it and I'll stand here and watch. It would be a lot easier if you washed up after every meal, though.'

After much persuasion she got Ronnie to do the washing-up. He dropped and broke a couple of things, she suspected half on purpose. But it got done—and then he expected to be praised. Fair enough.

'Why don't you come to the day centre, Ronnie?' she asked then. 'We can arrange for you to be picked up, you get a nice meal and there's all sorts of activities there.'

'You know I went there once and I didn't like it. Lot of stuck-up people there who think they're better than me.'

'I'm sure that's not true. Why not give it another go? If you like, I'll come and go with you for the first visit, introduce you to a few people. What about next Friday?'

Graciously, Ronnie said that he'd think about it. She was to call in and he'd give her his decision.

'You'll really enjoy it Ronnie, I promise,' she said. Then she left. She had done what she could.

Her next visit was really different. Mrs Murphy— Olive—still lived in the little terraced house she'd moved into when she'd got married, fifty years before. It was spotless. The home help who'd been allocated to Olive had said that she was asked to make sure the front of the house was all right—the tiny flower-bed had to be weeded, the windows cleaned, the front step scrubbed. Appearances were important to Olive—they always had been.

Tania sat in the front room, waiting for her tea to be brought. Olive came in with a tray, complete with white traycloth. There were two cups and saucers, milk jug and sugar bowl, a teapot with a cosy, all in a pretty blue and white pattern. There were also a plate of biscuits, carefully arranged, and two side plates. Olive believed in standards.

They talked about the weather, the baby born next door (brought in, so Olive could hold her), what Olive had heard on the news. This was all absolutely necessary. Tania couldn't get down to business until the social conventions had been observed. But finally... 'You're still losing weight,' Tania said. 'You look a bit pale and you haven't shaken off that nasty cough. What did the doctor say, Olive?'

'He wants me to go into hospital for tests,' snapped Olive. 'And I told him there was no way I'd do that. Look at what happened to George!'

Tania knew what had happened to George. She had been told several times. Twenty years ago, before she'd started to lose her sight, George had gone into hospital for the most minor of operations. And he'd died. 'Just an adverse reaction to the anaesthetic,' the GP had told Tania. 'It couldn't have been expected and he got the very best of treatment. Sometimes it just happens, and we're all very sorry.'

But since that time Olive had maintained a deep suspicion of hospitals. 'I'd rather die in my own bed than go to one of them places,' she had told Tania.

'There's no need for you to die just yet,' Tania had said.

Now she had to try again. 'I really do think you

ought to consider it,' Tania said. 'I'd come with you, see you were settled all right.'

Olive's lips thinned. 'I'm not going to hospital,' she said.

The Golden Rule again. You could ask, suggest, try to persuade. But you couldn't make up other people's minds. 'Well, think about it,' Tania said.

She went back to her office before going on her afternoon call to Jonathan, and after working found time to call in at her little bedroom in the school and have a quick wash, put on fresh make-up. And some scent. She found some people responded better when she wore scent. Then she set off—quite early.

It was another very hot day. As she drove, the car window down, she thought about her next appointment. She was looking forward to it. Jonathan represented a challenge. But, then, so did all her work.

She was an honest woman. She had to admit to herself that she was looking forward to seeing Jonathan again because she was attracted to him. She liked his voice, his appearance, his sense of humour. The shock when she'd seen him for the first time was with her still.

Irritably, she reached and turned on her radio, turned it on loud. She had to think of something else. Jonathan Knight was a client, nothing more. Men of his kind weren't for her. He was tough, arrogant, super-masculine. Just the opposite of the kind of man she liked. She had to face it, Jonathan was the kind of man who could hurt her very easily, if she let him. Then, more irritated than ever, she turned the radio even louder.

Jonathan had a guest when she arrived, a short, grey-haired, older man with lively blue eyes. 'This is my good friend, Charles Forsythe,' Jonathan said. 'He's the neurosurgeon who will operate on me.'

Charles shook her hand. 'I'll leave you in peace in a minute,' he said. 'Just finish my tea first. May I pour you a cup?' So she sat with the two men to chat. After all, she was early.

'Charles has been describing the operation I'll have,' Jonathan said. 'I wanted to know everything about it.'

'Some of my clients don't want to know anything,' Tania said. 'They leave everything up to the professionals. It's as if not knowing anything means that nothing can go wrong. Others—like you—want to know everything. Then they're master of the situation. If things do go wrong, they know why.'

Charles smiled at her. 'That's a very exact description of how my patients behave,' he said. 'You're a very shrewd young lady. Now, I'll do some exploratory examinations on Jonathan in a couple of weeks. Computerised tomagraphy, then magnetic resonance imaging. We've done them already, of course, and I don't expect to find anything I don't already know. Then, a few weeks after that, we'll try to put things right. It'll be an all-or-nothing operation. Not a difficult one either, a junior surgeon could do it. We get into the skull and hope to find something causing pressure. If we're in luck, all will be well. Prayer is as much use as a surgeon's skill, because all we can do is remove pressure on the visual cortex or the optic nerve. If the neural pathways are severed or interrupted, there's nothing a surgeon can do. So Jonathan will either regain his sight at once—or he'll be blind for life.'

It was a bleak forecast—but she saw that this was the way Jonathan liked to hear things. 'I know my chances now,' he said. 'Now, Charles, tell me what the hospital gossip is. You were later than you said you'd be.'

Tania saw that Charles was a little uncomfortable. 'I had one of those cases,' he said. 'A young girl—nine years old. We didn't know exactly what we'd find until we opened her up. It started as a spinal case, but we found a tumour that had spread and spread and we had to chase it all over her lower body. With any luck we'll have taken it all out—but the poor thing will have a body that's a mass of scars.'

Tania couldn't help it. She said nothing but Jonathan noticed her sudden gasp of horror. 'Has that upset you, Tania?' he asked.

'It's just that nine years old seems very young,' she said. 'She has to grow up… When she's older, when she wants to wear her first bikini, she'll be desolate.'

'When she's a bit better I'm going to get our plastics man to look at her,' Charles said. 'We won't just abandon her, Tania.'

When Charles had gone she started to teach Jonathan a little about cooking. First there was the arrangement of things he might need—how to navigate through his fridge-freezer and his cupboards, how to arrange the pans he might need. He had a gas hob and an electric oven, and she showed him how to deal with them.

Usually she took these steps very slowly. Her clients needed to learn practical skills, but at the same time they were having to come to terms with their disability. It wasn't uncommon for people to appear to be doing very well, and then, without notice, to burst into tears.

But Jonathan wasn't like that. He appeared to be able to thrust his feelings behind him, to concentrate on the matter in hand. She thought there was something almost inhuman about his concentration. He listened, he tried, and when he made a mistake he repeated the action till he got things right. And so he learned.

He told her he liked boiled eggs. She watched as he took two eggs from the fridge, put them in a pan and covered them with water, waited until he could tell that the water was boiling and then set a timer to ring after three and a half minutes. Then he put bread in the toaster and buttered it when it sprang up.

'Would you care to join me in toast and a boiled egg, Miss Richardson?' he invited.

'I'd be delighted, Dr Knight,' she replied. They sat at the table in the kitchen and ate their eggs.

He told her he preferred cafetière coffee. She was showing him how to pour in exactly the right amount of boiling water without scalding himself when there was a ringing sound from the living room.

'My mobile! I left it on the coffee-table. I'll get it, Tania.' He stood, felt his way to the door then strode purposefully forward before she could warn him. A half-second later there was a crash and the sound of a body hitting the floor.

'Jonathan!'

She found him stretched full length on the floor, an overturned chair showing what he had fallen over. Quickly she knelt, reached for his head to—

'Don't touch me!' She leapt backwards. He didn't need to shout at her!

She watched him push himself onto his hands and knees and stand upright. She saw by the white face that he was in pain, possibly also angry—very angry. Joe had told her that he had developed a temper, she remembered.

'Have you hurt yourself?' she asked.

'Yes. Don't offer me sympathy—it was my own fault. I moved too quickly. Sometimes I just forget things. You'd think that after two weeks of blindness I'd be getting used to it.'

The mobile phone was still ringing. She saw him turn towards the sound, but noticed that there were two more chairs and the coffee-table in his way.

'I'll get it,' she said. 'For the moment you just move very slowly and try to work out what's in your way.'

For a moment she thought that he was going to refuse. But then he cautiously felt forward, and she ran to where she could see the mobile phone—on the bookshelf. She took it to him.

'Hello… Joe… Mrs Cullen. Yes, of course I remember her, the lady with… She was given what?'

It was nothing to do with her, she wasn't to blame, but Tania cringed at the anger in Jonathan's voice.

'Right…right… Yes, it's a risk but give her a double dose. And if it doesn't work, ring me right back. Now, Joe, get me the sister on the line… Yes, I am angry and I don't care if I should be taking things easy. Get me the sister on the line!'

There was a pause. Tania looked at his hunched body, the blackness of his expression and decided not to interfere. This wasn't her business—besides, he frightened her.

His voice was quiet at first—the lull before the storm. 'Ah, Sister Elland, Dr Knight here. Now, I gather one of my patients, Mrs Cullen, has been given 100 mg tablets instead of 10 mg tablets. Quite a difference, I'm sure you'll agree. Would you like to explain it? No, that will not do as an excuse. The new nurse didn't do something wrong, the new nurse shouldn't have been allowed near the patient, unsupervised. She's there to learn, not to cover for you while you sit in your office and read magazines. Now, this is the last time this will happen. Once more, and you're out of my ward, out of the hospital and you won't be a nurse any more, much less a sister. *Do I make myself clear?*' And suddenly his voice was back to normal. 'Good, I'm glad you understand that.'

He clicked off the mobile and there was silence in the room.

'Partly I'm angry because I've lost my sight,' he said eventually. 'I wouldn't have shouted before. But that woman deserved everything I said. I don't like it when things go wrong.'

'Nobody does. But you're going to have to control your temper. If you act suddenly, impulsively, when you're blind you can be a danger both to yourself and other people.'

'That's going to be hard!'

She had to say it. 'There's nothing more comic than a blind person losing his temper. He looks ridiculous.'

For a moment she thought she had gone too far. But when Jonathan spoke it was another half-understood cry for help. 'Do all blind people feel as helpless and as impotent as I do?'

'Many do at first,' she said quietly, 'but they tend to come to an accommodation in time.'

Tania could sense his frustration. 'An accommodation? In time? Just excuse me a minute,' he said, and pulled off the T-shirt he was wearing, today a dark blue one. She looked at him with apprehension. Now what?

Something, a reaction to frustration she had never come across before. He crouched, stretched full length on the polished floor, his hands underneath him. Then he pushed downwards slowly, raising his body. Press-ups. She had seen the PE teacher in the school doing them with the bigger, stronger boys. But never like this.

At first he moved slowly, so that she could see the muscles in his arms and shoulders quiver with the strain. Then he moved quickly, his chest appearing to bounce off the floor. She lost count when he passed thirty repetitions. Now she could hear the rasping in his throat as he dragged in great sobbing breaths and the sweat gathered in a sheen on his back and dripped from his hair. Eventually he had to slow down, and she could see the agony in his face as he forced the tortured muscles to do just one, two, three more repetitions. And finally he was done. With a groan he collapsed on the floor.

'You'd better go for a shower,' she said.

He was calmer after his shower. He changed into fresh chinos and shirt and suggested they go back to work in the kitchen. Tania was amazed! She had never had a client like this before. But he wanted to do more. 'Boiled eggs are fine to start with,' he said, 'but how about grilling bacon?'

'Difficult,' Tania said, 'much, much more difficult.'

They were trying to cope with the grill when the intercom rang. 'I'll take care of things here if you want to answer it,' Tania said. 'If there's anything I can do, call me.'

He was back a few moments later; she couldn't read the expression on his face. Previously he had been en-grossed in learning, now he seemed half amused, half irritated.

'I have a visitor,' he said, 'my senior registrar, Eleanor Page. She's called to see if I'm all right.'

'Well, I'd better go, then,' said Tania. She could

have done without this interruption—the work had been going well.

'You'll do no such thing. I have to learn and your time is valuable. I'll just let her in.'

Eleanor was in her early thirties, a glacial blonde with expensive clothes, expensive make-up, expensive jewellery. Tania thought her perfume was a bit excessive. Jonathan was blind. His other senses were in perfect order. Then she wondered why she was disliking the woman so quickly. On the other hand, any dislike seemed to be mutual. Tania caught the quick assessing glance, the momentarily pursed lips as Eleanor sized her up. She sees me as a rival, Tania thought, and felt a little more cheerful.

After introducing the two, Jonathan explained that this was his tuition time. Eleanor would have to sit quietly and not interrupt while Tania taught him.

'Fine by me,' Eleanor said, obviously wishing to appear agreeable. 'I'll just sit here quietly and watch.' And for a while she did.

After twenty minutes Tania was feeling a bit embarrassed. She suggested that Jonathan make them all a cafetière of coffee and they sat down together.

'Certainly,' Jonathan said, 'but we only break for ten minutes.'

'If there's anything you want to discuss about work,' Tania went on desperately, 'anything confidential, then I could sit here in the kitchen while you—'

'Well, that would be kind—' Eleanor started.

At exactly the same time Jonathan said, 'No need for that at all. We'll all have coffee together.'

So they had coffee together. Jonathan told Eleanor what Charles had said to him. Eleanor had been away on a course for a week and didn't know the latest de-

velopments. She was very supportive, and absolutely
certain that Jonathan would regain his sight. When she
said so she leaned over, rested her hand on his knee
and left it there. After a moment Jonathan moved his
leg. Then they chatted about work for a little.

When Jonathan said it was time to start work again,
Eleanor said that she had better go, she had work to
do, too. She kissed Jonathan—for quite a long time,
Tania thought. Then she went to the door. As she did
so, she beckoned for Tania to follow her.

This was Jonathan's home. Tania wasn't having his
guests making secret signs to her just because he
couldn't see. And it seemed like betraying the confidence of a client. 'Did you want to talk to me,
Eleanor?' she asked out loud.

Quickly Eleanor managed to mask her evident fury.
'Just a quick word if you don't mind,' she said.
'Jonathan, it's girl talk—is that all right?'

'Be my guest,' he said airily. 'I'll be in the kitchen.'

'I just want you to know how much I care for
Jonathan,' Eleanor said when they were alone. 'I was
devastated when this happened—but I don't think it
does any good showing him that, does it?'

'Not much,' Tania agreed.

'You know he was injured pushing me out of the
way of a falling ladder? If he hadn't done that he
wouldn't have been blinded.'

Just for a moment Tania thought she saw real feelings in Eleanor, a terror of what might have happened
to her and a feeling of guilt that Jonathan had suffered
instead of her. She felt a moment's sympathy.

Eleanor went on, 'The point is, we're close. We're
very…very good friends.'

'Lovers?' Tania asked bluntly.

Eleanor seemed pleased that Tania had brought it up. 'Yes. Please, don't tell him that I told you, he'd be so embarrassed and angry—but, yes, we're lovers. The trouble is, recently things have been a bit, well, difficult between us. I thought we were getting things together again but…this accident couldn't have come at a worse time. I don't care whether he's blind or not, but he seems to want to keep me at a distance. What I'd like to ask you, Tania, is…will you keep an eye on him for me? If there's anything at all I can do, get in touch with me?'

'Well, I won't report on him,' Tania replied evenly, 'but certainly, if there's any way you can be of help, I'll let you know.'

Eleanor decided to make the most of a bad job. 'You're so kind, Tania. Must fly now.' And she was gone.

Tania stood there for a full minute, trying to decide how she felt.

The kitchen now smelled wonderfully of grilling bacon. But that wasn't what Tania wanted to talk about. 'I could have left you alone with Eleanor for a few minutes,' she said reproachfully to Jonathan. 'After all, she did make the effort to come to see you. Why were you rotten to her?'

'Eleanor is all right if you know how to handle her. Now, tell me, what did she tell you that you were to keep from me?'

'How d'you know she told me to keep anything from you?'

'Because you can't tell lies, or I'm learning to detect them. There was something in your voice that said that you were trying to keep a secret. And I know Eleanor from way back. She loves intrigue. A very good doctor, by the way.'

'She's also very attractive,' Tania said.

'I know. And I love beautiful women, I always have. Now, Eleanor, let me guess… Did she tell you that we were lovers?'

Tania said nothing for a while. 'I think you ought to turn over that bacon.'

'Your silence tells me what I want to know,' he said cheerfully. 'Eleanor told you we were lovers.'

'Your private life is no concern of mine,' said Tania. 'Now, please, can we drop the subject? I'm your re-habilitation worker, not your confessor. I don't need…I don't want to hear about your love life. My job is help-ing you to cope with being blind.'

'Quite so,' said Jonathan.

Tania wondered why she felt so displeased with life.

It was more time than she usually gave to one of her clients, but Tania juggled her appointments, worked late a couple of evenings and discovered that she could see Jonathan in another two days—a Friday afternoon. When he saw this in her schedule Derrick was suspi-cious.

'Ronnie Slack in the morning—that's fine,' he said. 'But you're seeing more of this Dr Knight than is nec-essary. Is he a difficult case?'

'Just the opposite. He's a pleasure to work with.' She remembered something and said slyly, 'You told me I had to do my best for this man. Well, that's what I'm doing. Incidentally, I've met the neurologist. Charles Forsythe. He's a very nice man.'

'I see. Well, don't neglect your other cases.'

So Tania went to see Jonathan and once again he

was the perfect pupil. 'You work so hard, you're spoiling me for everyone else I see,' she told him. 'I want them to be all like you.'

'You haven't known me long. I'm keeping my bad habits hidden for a while.'

'Not hidden well enough. I've seen your temper and I—' The intercom sounded.

He went to answer it, when he came back into the room he looked disturbed. 'There's a man outside who claims to be your boss,' he said. 'Name's Derrick Gee. Says he assessed me a week or so ago—though I don't remember it.'

'He is my boss,' Tania said doubtfully, 'and technically I suppose he's entitled to see how I'm getting on. But he hasn't been to see me work since I started.'

'We'd better let him in, then.'

After a couple of minutes it was obvious what Derrick wanted. He wanted to spy and he wanted his department to make a good impression on Charles Forsythe. 'I trust Miss Richardson's work is satisfactory, Dr Knight?'

'More than satisfactory, Mr Gee. When she's allowed to get on with it.'

'And we can count on a good report to Mr Forsythe?'

'Charles Forsythe will make up his own mind. He always does.'

Derrick didn't seem to notice that he was being snubbed, that he was irritating Jonathan. 'Well, I'm pleased that my department is doing its best for you.'

The intercom sounded again. Tania wondered if this would anger Jonathan further, but he went as he always did to answer it. 'The florist,' he said when he returned.

'Perhaps we should have a look,' Derrick said ingratiatingly. 'There are some strange people about and you're not yet—'

'I said it was the florist. He's been here before, I recognised his voice. Tania, perhaps you'd give me a hand with whatever he's bringing up.'

Now Derrick did realise he wasn't wanted. But all he could do was smoulder in silence as Jonathan went to open the door.

Tania went with him and took the flowers from him. He reached in his pocket for coins, identified them as she had shown him by rubbing his thumb round the edge, and then tipped the man.

'You're doing well,' she said briefly. 'These are glorious flowers—why don't you smell them?' So he buried his head in the bunch. She looked at them. They had been picked with care—all of them were scented. 'Someone's very thoughtful,' she added.

They went back into the living room and Jonathan said, 'I've got three vases and they're all in a cupboard in the kitchen. Why don't I fetch one, half fill it with water then you can help me put these in it?'

Tania was pleased. He was learning to think and to plan for himself.

When he had gone Derrick came over and plucked an envelope from the flowers. 'Someone will have to read this for him,' he said, and opened it. 'It says "With all my love and all good wishes for a quick recovery. I'll be in touch, Meryl Chandler." She's that television actress, you know. A famous beauty. Obviously there's something going on between them.'

'He has a lot of beautiful friends,' said Tania.

Jonathan came back with the vase, and Tania helped him slide the flowers into it. Then Derrick grumpily announced that he ought to be going and that Jonathan should feel free to phone him at any time, no matter how trivial the reason. Jonathan assured him that there was nothing to worry about, Miss Richardson was doing an excellent job. Derrick left.

'I don't think I've made a new friend,' Jonathan said when he'd gone. 'But, there again, neither has he. Not a gracious man.'

'His is a difficult job,' Tania said. She felt she ought to defend her boss. Well, just a little. 'He's got the usual bureaucratic problems. Not enough resources and too much work.'

'He should look for grace under pressure. You've got it. Now, was there a card with these flowers?'

She didn't have time to feel pleased with his compliment. She had to read the card to him.

'From Meryl! Well, that's very nice of her.' He smelt the flowers again. 'Very nice indeed.'

'I've seen her on television,' Tania said cautiously, 'in that play about Catherine the Great. She's absolutely beautiful.'

'So she is. I used to see a lot of her when I worked in London, and we parted good pals.'

'You *do* like beautiful women, don't you?'

'I do. I told you that earlier. Are you beautiful, Tania? You have a beautiful name.'

'I think beauty is in the soul, the spirit, the mind, not the face.'

'You may be right. I'm learning that through being blind. My other senses are getting more acute. D'you know, when I was in Charles's ward, there was an absolutely gorgeous nurse who used to come and read to me. She was gorgeous because of her voice, Tania. And if I get my sight back, and she turns out to be not what other people think of as a raving beauty, then I shall still think of her as beautiful. Because she is.'

'That's nice,' Tania said, 'but would you take her out if she turned out to be…rather plain? Could she ever become your girlfriend?'

Jonathan's smile was sheepish. 'Probably not,' he said, 'and I know that doesn't show me in a very good light.' He shrugged. 'But you're avoiding my question. Are you beautiful, Tania? You don't have to boast. Just tell me whether other people think of you as beautiful.'

'I would like you to think of me as beautiful in the same way you thought that nurse was gorgeous. If what I say and what I do for you is helpful then that's a kind of beauty.'

'And so it is.' He persisted, 'But are you beautiful?'

'People have said that I am…quite good-looking.'

In fact, she knew that she was beautiful. When she entered a room she could feel the current of interest from men as they observed her. And the men she'd had to discourage!

Her hair was dark, falling nearly to her shoulders. It was her one concession to vanity to keep it long. Her brown eyes were large—but so was her mouth. Once, many years ago, a boy had told her that it was generous, and kissable, and beautifully curved. In those days she'd believed things like that. She used little make-up, but her skin glowed with health. And her figure was good. No, it was more than good, it was marvellous. Other women envied her slim body, high breasts, proud neck. She knew that if he could see her, Jonathan would think her beautiful. But then…

She wasn't sure where this conversation was going. She felt she was embarking on topics she had never had to deal with before—and it was disturbing her. But exciting her as well.

'May I feel your face?' he asked suddenly, 'Perhaps your shoulders, too? Please, say no if you're at all worried but I want to see if I can get a picture of you through my hands.'

She hesitated only a moment. 'All right,' she said, 'so long as you don't try to take advantage.' Then she laughed. 'I know you won't. It's usually the old men who try—they forget themselves.'

'I'm not an old man yet. Let me feel your hair first.'

Other people had asked to do this. But this man was different. His hands were very gentle. He lifted her long hair, let it sweep through his fingers. He trailed the tips down her cheeks, caressed the corners of her mouth so that it almost tickled. Whatever it was doing for him, it was giving her pleasure. He gently felt the muscles of her shoulders, ran his fingers down her arms. Then, abruptly, he let go of her. And she was sorry.

'I liked that,' he said, 'and I especially like your long hair. But I can't tell whether you're beautiful or not.'

His voice was slightly agitated. His mood had changed completely. Tania wasn't too upset. Rapid mood changes were a common feature of people who had just suffered a trauma like this man had.

'It's nearly five on Friday afternoon,' he said. 'Joe will be coming round soon. In the past, nearly every Friday he used to call round and we'd go for a run together. Hell, what I wouldn't give for a run! Press-ups are fine, but I need to stretch my legs.' The intercom buzzed. 'That'll be Joe,' he said. Tania smiled.

'In that case, how would you like to go running with him?'

*   *   *

She was spending far too much time with Jonathan. She should have left at five. But here she was, an hour later, standing at the edge of a lonely flat beach with two men dressed in running kit in front of her.

She took a thick bandage and loosely tied Joe's wrist to Jonathan's. 'You'll have to get used to each other's pace,' she said. 'Move very slowly at first. Jonathan, this beach is very flat, there's hardly anything to trip over. But try and pick up your feet a little more than you usually would. Now, start with just a jog trot, run to the edge of the sea and then come back to me.'

Joe grinned at her delightedly. 'This is brilliant,' he said. 'Tania, you're a genius.'

Jonathan said nothing, but moved his head, as if trying to sense which way he was to go. 'Let's try it,' he said.

She watched as they ran away from her. At first they had difficulty, unable to adapt to each other's pace or arm movements. But after a while they picked up a rhythm and she could tell that they were moving more easily together.

They reached the edge of the sea, turned and ran back to her. 'You're doing well now,' she said. 'You're on your own for half an hour. Just remember, Joe, keep away from the softer sand—you can trip in that. Oh, and Jonathan's been in hospital for a stay—he's not as fit as he thinks.'

'Yes, miss,' said Jonathan.

'Off you go, then.'

She watched the two figures dwindle away into the distance. But she knew they'd come back.

CHAPTER THREE

ON MONDAY morning there was a message on Tania's desk. Could she call at Derrick's office? She didn't go at once—there were a couple of letters to write, her log to fill in, a phone call to make. But eventually there was no reason to put it off any longer, so she went to see him. She suspected that no good would come of the meeting.

But Derrick was affable. He gave her a glass of iced orange juice, asked her if she'd thought further about the full-time post, told her that he'd received excellent reports on her work from a couple of doctors.

'We work best if we work together,' he said. 'You're the newest of our rehabilitation workers, I know all the others well. I really think you and I should get together some time in a more relaxed atmosphere. What about a drink tonight?'

'I'm busy tonight,' she said. 'But I know two or three of the others are going to the King's Arms this lunchtime. We could join them if you like.'

He shook his head. 'No. I think we need to be alone together. Just the two of us. I'm free every evening this week—when are you free?'

She would have to spell it out to him. Again. 'Derrick, we work together. In fact, I work for you. I don't think that relationships that start at work are ever successful, so I decided a long time ago that I would never go out with anyone I worked with.'

It wasn't the answer he'd wanted. 'Of course, you're

entitled to your point of view,' he said sourly, 'though I don't think it's a correct one.'

He picked up a pen, tapped it on his desk in a rhythm that she found distracting. 'Having a relationship with someone you work with *may* be foolish,' he said. 'Having a relationship with someone you work *for*—with a client, in effect—is certainly foolish.'

He had irritated her so she would provoke him. 'I thought our first responsibility as rehabilitation workers was to establish a relationship?'

'A professional one! You know what I'm talking about, Tania.'

'I'm not sure I do. Have you anything specific to complain about in my relationships with any of my clients?'

This time he didn't respond. 'Not at all,' he said. 'I'm sure I can rely in every way on your professionalism and good sense.'

She went back to her desk, picked up her bag and went out to visit Olive Murphy.

That afternoon Tania called on Jonathan again. They would work more in the kitchen.

'You're upset,' he said after a while. 'You're doing a good job but you're not concentrating and there's something else on your mind. Want to tell me what it is?'

'No. I'm here to help you, not have you help me. And it's only a little problem. A work problem. I'll sort it out.'

'Didn't you tell me that the best thing to do with problems was get them into the open? Let's do just that.'

So she told him. 'I have this client, Olive Murphy.

She's eighty, as bright as a button, suffering from chronic glaucoma. It could have been treated but…Olive isn't fond of the medical profession and it's now too late. With a bit of help she can live comfortably in the house she's been in for the past fifty years.'

'No family?'

'None at all. Her husband's dead, they never had children. The family next door are supportive but they have young children and they can't do too much.'

'So what's the problem?'

'I think she's ill,' said Tania. 'In fact, I think she's very ill and she won't accept any help. Her GP is a young woman—younger than me, in fact. She tries her best but Olive just won't listen to her. I'm quite close to Olive, but she won't listen to me either. All we want is for her to go to hospital, have a few tests.'

'Doesn't seem much to ask,' Jonathan agreed. 'I see a lot of old ladies in my clinics who—'

The shock hit him suddenly, hard. 'No,' he managed to grate out, 'I used to see a lot of old ladies.'

Once again, this was something Tania had met before. One of her clients would be engrossed in something, and suddenly reality would hit them. They were blind. For a moment they had forgotten, now the horror came back. It was hard.

Tania said nothing, just reached over and took Jonathan's hand. He squeezed it for a second, then carefully released her grip and laid her hand back on her lap.

'Sorry,' he said. 'I should concentrate on what I'm saying.' She looked at his bleak expression and decided not to comment.

He went on, 'As I said, I used to see a lot of old ladies, and quite often they enjoyed a trip out to the hospital. They get a cup of tea and a nurse makes a fuss of them.'

'Olive is different. Her husband died in hospital—one of those unfortunate cases. He was allergic to the anaesthetic or something. It was only a minor operation. And since then Olive has never trusted a hospital, or doctors either.'

'Hmm. Tell me her symptoms—as best you can describe them.'

So she did and instantly Jonathan turned into a doctor. She knew he was a doctor, of course, everyone had told her so. But it was interesting to watch his brooding face, try to answer the detailed questions he asked. And, subtly, their relationship changed. No longer was she his tutor. They were equals—or she was even learning from him.

'I want to meet her,' he said when he had finished. 'Can you take me round to her house? She might object to doctors—but she'll think that a blind person can't do much harm. But I don't want to intrude.'

'Olive loves visitors. But I'm supposed to be helping you, not you helping me.'

'Taking me there will be helping me. It'll give me the chance to feel useful again.'

'We-ell,' she mumbled, 'I'd like to take you—but I'm supposed to be training you. I don't think Derrick Gee would think much of it. And he might be right.'

'What Derrick Gee thinks doesn't really concern me.'

He'd meant that, she could tell. There was that flash of…self-confidence that she thought had once been such a great part of his character.

'Tell you what,' he said, 'we can compromise. I'll go with you to see this Olive for a while. Then you stay on this afternoon after five. I think I might need a companion, and you would be just right. I'm having a visitor and you would help me cope.'

Tania said nothing, thinking about it. He misinterpreted her silence. 'Of course, you might have plans,' he said. 'I don't want to interfere with your life outside work.'

'I don't have much life outside work,' she told him, and then wished she hadn't.

'Not a lot of life outside work? No boyfriend?' When she didn't answer, he went on, 'Sorry, that was a personal question and I shouldn't have asked.'

'I'll answer it. No, at the moment I haven't got a boyfriend. But I'm not going to go into any more detail than that. And, yes, I would like you to come to see Olive and, yes, I will stay behind after five o'clock.'

'All settled, then. Let's go to see Olive.' Then he frowned. 'I'll fetch something.'

When he came back he was carrying the traditional doctor's little black bag. 'Tools of my trade,' he told her, snapping the case open. 'But a lot of them I don't think I can use. Could a blind man use a hypodermic syringe?'

'Yes,' she said. 'Some of our clients suffer from diabetes, and blindness isn't uncommon in diabetics. Many of them manage to inject themselves.'

'I see. The more I talk to you, Tania, the more I realise that in some ways I'm lucky.'

Olive looked even weaker than she had that morning. Tania saw her pale face and worried. But Olive had visitors and was delighted with them. She made more tea and fussed round Jonathan, making sure he had everything he needed. 'You can feel the difference be-

tween digestive and Garibaldi biscuits,' she told him.
'Just squeeze them a little.'

He had told her he was a doctor, said he was now
just getting used to having lost his sight. 'You could
help me, Olive. Tania here says you've not been feeling
too well recently. Could I try to examine you? See if
I can still do it? Tania will stay here and help me.'

'Just so long as you don't want me to go to hospital,'
Olive said darkly. 'That is out of the question.'

First he asked her about how she was feeling, her
diet, her sleeping, her bathroom habits. Then he managed to listen to her chest, and with Tania's help took
her blood pressure and temperature. Finally he put his
instruments away. 'You're ill, Olive. You must have
more tests.'

Olive knew what that meant. 'No,' she snapped. 'I'm
not going to hospital.'

Jonathan felt in his bag, then turned with a puzzled
expression to Tania. 'I think I've dropped a little box
of pills down the side of the seat in your car. Could
you go to have a look for me? I'm sorry to be a nui-
sance.'

She hadn't noticed him handling any box of pills but
she went anyway. Her car was parked some distance
away and as she paced along the hot street she thought
that this had been a waste of time. Olive wasn't going
to have her mind changed for her.

She pushed her fingers down the side of the seat but
didn't find the pills. A couple of sticky sweets she had
dropped, ninepence in copper coins—but no pills. Feeling irritated, she went back.

As she entered the little hall she could hear Jonathan
speaking. 'Now, you won't let me down, Olive? We
have decided on what's best, haven't we?'

'I suppose so, Doctor. Though what I'm going to say to Tania I just don't—'

'Take my word for it, Tania will be delighted. Now, do you think I might have another cup of tea? Just if there's one left in the pot.'

'I'm sure there is. Another biscuit?'

'You sent me for those pills to get me out of the room,' Tania said viciously. 'You never dropped anything, did you?'

They had left Olive and were driving back to Jonathan's flat.

'I didn't drop anything,' he admitted, 'and, yes, I did want you out of the room.'

'Dr Knight, you exceeded yourself. In this situation I was the professional, you were there as a helper. You might have undermined all that I've done. I've spent weeks trying to get Olive to trust me. And—'

'And we got the result you wanted. Incidentally, you were right. She is ill and she needs urgent medical attention.'

'Right!' Tania still felt irritated, but she had to admit that Jonathan had succeeded where she had failed. 'What did you say that I didn't? How did you persuade her?'

'This constant blackness has it rewards. There are things you can hear when you can't see. Olive is scared of being ill. But with you she's forced herself into a corner—she can't go to hospital and still have her pride. She's spent so much time telling you she won't go to hospital that she daren't back down. She wouldn't change her mind with you in the room. I told her I thought she was ill, that we could treat her. Then I asked her what she thought her husband would have wanted her to do. That convinced her.'

Tania was silent for a moment. 'Perhaps I've underestimated you,' she muttered.

When they got back to Jonathan's flat, he telephoned Olive's GP and asked her if it was all right for Olive to be admitted to hospital. Then he phoned Joe at the hospital, asking him to arrange an ambulance for Olive and an urgent appointment to see Eleanor in the clinic. 'She'll probably be admitted,' he finished, 'so see that there's a bed for her.'

He listened a moment longer, then laughed and said, 'Anything to keep working.' Then he hung up.

'Joe thinks it's wrong that I wander round the town, picking up patients,' he said. 'He says it's not only unethical but it's more work for him.'

'You really enjoyed seeing Olive, didn't you? It gave you a kick.'

'It's my job, it's what I do,' he said. Without changing inflection, he added, 'Or perhaps it's what I did.'

'Whatever happens, you'll still be a doctor,' Tania told him. 'You just couldn't stop. Now, we'll start from scratch. Make yourself a bacon sandwich. And I'll have one, too.'

As Jonathan cooked, moving carefully about the kitchen, they chatted casually about his work. She had never realised quite how interesting infectious diseases were. 'There's a book you can borrow,' he told her. 'Go and look in the spare bedroom, down the corridor. I think it's by the bed.'

She walked down the passage and opened the door. This was a room she had never visited before—and it amazed her. It was unlike all the other rooms in the flat. It was a woman's room.

The walls were a lovely rose pink, and the curtains matched. Neatly arranged bottles on the dressing-table were all of the very best. Behind the door was hanging a white silk night robe. Tania thought of her own old woollen dressing-gown and sniffed. There were pictures, ornaments, a pile of *Vogue*s and *Harpers' Bazaar*s. She didn't look in the built-in wardrobe but she knew it would be crammed with clothes.

So there was a woman in his life. And a woman of taste and style and money. Obviously Eleanor. Well, what had she expected?

The spare bedroom was next door. Tania found the book he had recommended and went back to the kitchen. Jonathan had the grill on too high and he hadn't replaced the bacon in the way she had taught him to. She told him to do things right, then snapped, 'Sorry, I went into the wrong bedroom. I didn't mean to pry.'

'That's all right,' he said calmly. 'This grill all right now? And if you ask me nicely, I'll tell you all about her.'

'Tell me all about who?' She couldn't help it. Her voice rose slightly.

'Tell you all about who the woman is whose bedroom you went into.'

'Eleanor explained that you're going through a bad patch now. I guess that's why she's not here. And you're entitled to see as many women as you like. I'm not in the least interested.'

'Rubbish! You've been icy and upset since you came back into this kitchen. You've judged me. Here, have a bacon sandwich.'

Reluctantly, she sat down at the table opposite him. 'It's nothing to me if you have a woman staying here. You're a free spirit.'

'Too right I am. But you wouldn't want me to ignore my poor old mum just because I've become a successful doctor?'

'Your what? Your poor old mum? That's not a mum's room—it's Eleanor's room. It's not the room of a—'

'It's not Eleanor's room, Tania. Eleanor has never spent a night in this flat. Do you want me to tell you about her?'

Well, yes, she did, quite desperately, but there was no way she was going to show her eagerness to him. 'You can tell me if you like,' she said, pretending indifference.

'Eleanor and I were lovers—some years ago when we both worked in London. Then it ended—amicably enough, I think. I got the job as Consultant here. After some time Eleanor applied to be my specialist registrar. I phoned her, said I didn't think it was a good idea after we'd been so close. She said that I was spoiling her career chances because of my own prejudices. We could work together, forget the past if I gave her the chance. She had quite a valid point.'

Tania was intrigued. 'So you gave her a job. Has she kept her half of the bargain?'

Jonathan shrugged. 'Up till recently,' he said. 'Then I had to take her home one night and she misconstrued a friendly kiss—'

'A friendly kiss! I'll bet!'

'It was. Tania, I assure you it was. And I've tried to convince her of this.'

She believed him. But why was she so pleased there

was nothing serious between him and Eleanor? 'Well, it's not much like a mum's room,' she said.

He grinned. 'Don't be agist, Tania. Mum might be getting on a bit but she likes to keep herself looking nice.'

'Honestly, is it your mum's room? I feel a bit…well, it's not my business, but I thought—'

'It's my mum's room. Incidentally, you told me earlier that you had no boyfriend at the moment. Well, I don't have a girlfriend.'

'Oh,' she said. 'This is a very professional bacon sandwich.'

'I've been well taught.'

'Your mum,' Tania said when the sandwiches had been eaten and the coffee poured, 'where is she now? And does she know about your accident?'

'Mum is working in New York. And I haven't told her that I'm blind.'

'Don't you think you ought to tell her? Don't you think she's entitled to know? We find that the family is very important when getting someone to come to terms with things.'

Jonathan sipped his coffee, his face dark. 'Enough people know already. They think about me differently, I can tell when I phone them. They speak differently, more slowly even. They think that I'm—'

'They think that you're handicapped,' she supplied. 'It doesn't feel good, does it, Jonathan? But I think you're missing the point. You should phone your mother and tell her. She's going to be really angry when she finds out, and she's going to be hurt that you didn't tell her at once. It doesn't matter that you're trying to save her pain—that pain is her right.'

'That pain is her right,' he echoed. 'What a curious

thing to say. But I think I believe you. I will phone her.'

'I got carried away,' she said. 'I'm sorry. I should have said that, above all, it's your decision.'

'All right, it's my decision. I've made it. But thanks for the help in coming to it, Tania.'

She wanted to talk about something else now. 'Who is it that's coming this evening, Jonathan? And how am I to help you to cope?'

'Ah. It's the woman who sent me the flowers—Meryl Chandler.'

'The actress and the beauty,' said Tania.

'Quite. Well, I want you to stay here to stop her feeling sorry for me. If I'm alone I'll be quite happy, but she won't see that. She'll see me as having been deserted and she'll start making mad plans for me that I want no part of.'

'So am I here as your rehabilitation worker?'

'Well, yes. And I'd really like a bit more than that. Could you pretend that we were lovers?'

She looked at him blankly. 'Certainly not! I'm happy to be here as your friend, but that is all. I will not pretend to be your lover!' Just saying the words made her catch her breath.

'Then we'll stick to what you want.'

'We certainly will,' Tania said forcefully.

Five minutes later she was looking out of the window when a very large white car pulled up outside. A grey-uniformed man came round to open the back door, out of which stepped a woman clad completely in white—white dress, white shoes, white hat. 'I think your friend has arrived,' said Tania.

In fact, Meryl was very pleasant. When Jonathan introduced Tania as his rehabilitation worker, Meryl smiled and said that Jonathan had always been lucky. Somehow he always surrounded himself with very attractive women. And even without his sight he could do it! Tania decided she liked the woman. She offered to make them all coffee.

'This is only a flying visit,' Meryl said. 'I'd love to take you out to dinner, but I've got a meeting in Manchester later this evening and then it's back to the big city. But I heard—and I wanted to see if there is anything I can do.'

'I'm doing fine,' said Jonathan. 'Friends and colleagues are being very supportive. And I've got Tania here who's teaching me how to be independent.'

'Darling, you don't need to be taught to be independent! Just the opposite. Learn to relax a little and let people do things for you.' She sipped her coffee, winked at Tania. 'Would you like to come to London and stay in my flat for a week or two? You could have the spare room.'

'Thank you but no. I have to persevere up here.'

'You've got lots of friends there who would like to call round. Half the good-looking women in television know you,' Meryl teased.

'Possibly. But I'm staying here.'

'That's fair enough.' When she spoke again Meryl wasn't joking any more. 'There is one thing I'd like you to consider seriously. I'm going to New York for a month in two days—in fact, I'll probably run into your mother. When I come back I'll be joining a friend's yacht for a cruise round the Greek Islands for a few days. Would you like to come with me?'

'I'd fall overboard,' he said. 'Meryl, it's good of you to ask me but right now it's the last thing I need.'

'Well, I asked. And the offer is always open. Tania, do you think I could have another coffee, my dear?'

Shortly after that Meryl had to go. She kissed Jonathan affectionately, and to Tania's surprise kissed her with equal affection. 'Look after the old grouch,' Meryl whispered in her ear, and when Tania looked at her she wasn't surprised to see a tear in her eye.

'It's obvious she's very fond of you,' she said to Jonathan when she'd watched Meryl climb into the big white car.

'We had some good times together. All over now, of course, though we're still friends.'

'I'm glad about that. And she knows your mother. Shouldn't you have warned her not to say anything about your…your accident?'

'Not necessary. I'm going to take your advice and phone my mother later. She'll probably panic and come rushing over here, but I suppose that's what mothers are for.'

Thoughtfully, Tania said, 'In families, when a child, say, loses her sight, often it's the fathers who panic, who just can't cope. Mothers know there's a job to be done and they get on with it.'

He frowned. 'I don't do much paediatric work,' he said, 'but I think I'd agree with you.'

She pondered a minute and then changed the subject. 'How come you know so many beautiful women? Don't answer if you think that's personal.'

'I grew up surrounded by beautiful women. Have you heard of Marianne Knight?'

'Of course I have! She was that famous 1960s model, she did those adverts for soap and for… She's not your mother?'

'Even famous models can have children,' he pointed out. 'And she had me.'

'Let me look at you!' Tania took his face in her hands, turning it towards the light. 'Yes, you've got the same lips. The same big…big…'

'Big eyes,' he supplied. 'Say it, I can take it.'

'Well, you do look like her. I've never met anyone who had a mother who was famous.'

Jonathan mused. 'She was a good mother, always had time for me. Never interested in drugs, didn't like drinking too much, wouldn't waste her money. Just the opposite of a flower child, in fact. Which is probably why she's still happy and working today.'

'So what about your father?' The question came out before she had time to think about it. And it wasn't a good one.

He scowled. 'I never knew my father. Apparently Mother didn't know him for long. When I was twenty-one she offered to tell me his name, said I was entitled to know if I wanted. But I didn't. He'd paid no attention to me for all that time. I wasn't going to look him up now.'

'I see. But it must have been a hard decision.' Once again she came up against this hardness in Jonathan. He was tough.

'It was the 1960s. My mother had quite a lot of male friends.'

'So you decided to have a lot of female friends?'

She'd said the wrong thing again. 'Don't try to psychoanalyse me, Tania,' he snapped. 'I live my life the way I want to.'

'Of course,' she said.

CHAPTER FOUR

IT WAS three days before Tania could see Jonathan again. She had other cases—another nine, in fact—and other calls on her time. But when she went she felt— well, excited. Life was never dull when she was teaching Jonathan.

So, she was looking forward to seeing him. But she wasn't expecting that thrill that seemed to gather in a knot in her chest when she saw his tall, smiling figure. What was wrong with her?

'I've got some good news for you,' he said. 'Well, I think it's good news. You know we admitted Olive Murphy? Apparently, she's thoroughly enjoying being in hospital. The nurses think she's wonderful. And Eleanor has diagnosed what's wrong. It's what I suspected—Olive has tuberculosis.'

'Tuberculosis! But I thought that had died out…'

He sighed. 'So did we all. I'll tell you more about it later. But this time we've caught it in time and it can be treated. Olive will go home again in time.'

'That's marvellous! Jonathan, you're wonderful. Thank you so much!' On impulse she threw her arms round his neck, reached up and kissed him. A real kiss, a proper kiss, not on the cheek but on the lips. And then he kissed her back. His arms slipped round her, held her to him and she tightened her grasp on him. It was so sweet to kiss and be kissed like this. Their bodies were pressed together. She closed her eyes and let herself enjoy sensations that had been denied her for so long. But then…

'Jonathan,' she muttered, and pushed him away. He let her go at once.

'I'm sorry,' he said. 'I guess I got carried away a little.'

'It wasn't your fault, it was mine. I got carried away too and, well, it's just not proper, is it?'

He didn't reply at once. Then he said, 'No, perhaps it isn't proper.' There was another pause and then he said, in an entirely natural voice, 'What are you going to teach me today? May I say that I've practised with the boiled eggs and bacon sandwiches and now I'm an expert.'

'We're starting on mobility,' she said, 'beginning with long cane training. I think you're confident enough now. We've got the use of a church hall, it's about fifteen minutes' drive away.'

'So let's go. If I'm with you I do feel confident.'

Tania looked up at his face and blushed. 'Just one thing first,' she said. 'Keep still.' From her pocket she took a tissue and wiped his face. 'Lipstick,' she explained uncomfortably.

'Oh. I thought it was going to be something nice.'

When they arrived at the church hall she led Jonathan inside. 'I recognise the smell,' he said. 'I've been in so many places like this.'

'It's used a lot at night but we can have it most mornings and afternoons. It's just what we need. Now, this is your long cane. It's not the old-fashioned white stick, it's far more useful than that, but it is coloured white. Hold it here like this, wrap the strap round your wrist and point it towards the floor in front of you.'

He did as she told him. 'I've seen people using these before,' he said. 'Now I really feel blind.'

'You are blind,' she retorted. 'Now, don't go all helpless on me, you're my best pupil.'

She showed him how to hold the stick, how to walk slowly, waving the stick in front of him, sometimes touching the ground to show that there is nothing in front of him, that there was somewhere to put his feet. 'Now, walk across the hall,' she said. 'At the far end there's a wooden stage. When your cane touches it, stop.'

Tania knew this was hard for him. Other blind people had told her how hard it was to walk into the apparent unknown, without a wall to trail or a friend to hold onto. But he set off—slowly as she'd instructed. And when his cane rapped against the stage he stopped. Then he slid a foot forward till that, too, was against the stage. Then he felt for the edge of the stage with his hand. 'A stage,' he said. 'I would say about three feet high.' He knocked it with his knuckles. 'Bare wood and probably needs dusting.'

'Don't get smart with me, Knight,' she told him. 'Now, turn round and come back here. It's a wall in front of you this time.'

Jonathan was a quick study. After a while she put chairs in his way, made him detect them and walk round them. Then she made him walk along a wall, tapping it regularly to ensure he didn't move too far away. 'Very useful when you're in town,' she said. 'Make sure you don't wander off the edge of the pavement.'

She knew it was hard work and it was hot in the church hall. After an hour, in spite of his protests, she made him sit down and fetched them both a glass of water.

'Enjoying it?' she asked as they sat companionably on the edge of the stage.

'It's something new. And I'm sure you know, Tania, it's tremendously hard. What seems to be the simplest thing isn't simple. And I'm always convinced that there's something right in front of me that I'm going to bang into. Will I ever get confident about doing this?'

It was couched as a casual question, but she recognised the need for reassurance underneath. 'You'll be surprised how quickly you get confident,' she told him.

There were steps up the side of the stage. She taught him how to use the cane to feel for them, how to know exactly where to put his feet. This was harder. But he persevered and eventually he was moving faster and faster. 'Slowly,' she called. 'You're not using your cane now. You've memorised the steps, that's not the aim of the exercise.'

Soon it would be time to go. She took him onto the stage. 'Now, this is hard, this is dangerous,' she told him. 'You're facing the edge of the stage. Walk towards it…very, very slowly, using the cane to find the way. When your cane tells you that there's nowhere to go—stop. And, Jonathan, if I tell you to stop, do so at once.'

This time she followed Jonathan closely, ready to grab him if necessary. But it wasn't. He found the edge of the stage, stood still as he rapped his cane along the edge, and then said, 'I'm about eighteen inches away.'

'Perfect. We'll do it again.'

At first Tania had him approaching the edge of the stage at right angles. But then she moved him so he was approaching at a shallower angle. This was much more difficult and she saw the tiny beads of sweat shining at the edge of his hair. But he persevered. And he managed it.

'You've done really well,' she said eventually. 'One more time and then we'll call it a day. You must be tired.'

'One more time, then.' But this time, when he reached the edge of the stage he didn't stop. Instead, he turned sideways and walked along the edge, tapping his cane along the overhang to make sure he didn't fall off.

'Jonathan!' screamed Tania. 'Jonathan, stop now. You'll fall off, you're not up to that yet. Jonathan. Stop! You've come to the corner of the stage!'

He stopped then, and tapped a wide circle in front of him. 'Oh, no, I haven't,' he said.

But by this time she had walked to him, taken his arm and dragged him away from the edge. 'Jonathan! You're getting too confident! You have to take things easy at first. If you have an accident it'll put you back so far!'

He thought about that. 'I suppose you're right,' he said. 'I just like to get on with things.'

'You'll get on with things better if you take them at the right speed! Now, we're going back to the flat.'

Quite often there were setbacks when she was training people. She'd taught herself to be patient, to make allowances, not ever to get angry. Yet now her heart was beating quickly and she felt a quite unreasonable annoyance. Was this man different to any of the others?

'I enjoyed this,' he said. 'When do we do it again?'

'As soon as I can get away. And I'd like you to

practise finding your way around the flats—just in the gardens, though.'

'Good. We're making progress.'

She wondered exactly what she was progressing towards.

On the way back to the flat she stopped at a small shopping centre. 'Just going to get a box of chocolate ginger for Olive,' she told him. 'She loves it. Won't be a minute. I'm calling in at your ward tonight.'

'We're at Shelley's Chocolate Shop,' he guessed. 'Next door is the bookshop and then there's a ladies hairdresser's. I come here a lot myself.'

'You've got a good memory. That'll be very useful. I won't be long.'

But Tania was longer than she'd anticipated. Someone was ordering a speciality box and it took quite a time. And when she got back to her car—the little gold-wrapped box under her arm—Jonathan was gone. The car was locked.

What now? This was quite a busy road, but at the moment there were only a few people on the street. She looked up and down—no sign of Jonathan. He must have gone round a corner. What had happened? Had he been kidnapped?

She realised she was thinking foolishly. The road curved a few yards to her left—he might have turned the corner. So she ran—and there he was. He was quite safe. The relief was intense.

He was safe, he was smiling, the white cane held nonchalantly in his hand. Swiftly her relief turned to anger then apprehension. Jonathan was talking to Derrick. Where had he come from? She walked up to the two men.

'I'm surprised to see you out of the car,' she said to

Jonathan, trying but not succeeding in keeping the anger out of her voice.

He smiled at her. 'I'm sorry if I frightened you. But the sun was shining, there were few people about, I know this street very well and I just felt adventurous. So I tapped my way along the kerb a way. Here are the car keys, by the way.' He handed them to her.

This did nothing to calm her. 'How come you're here?' she asked Derrick ungraciously.

Derrick was cool. 'I came to the church hall to see how you were getting on. Obviously I only missed you by a minute so I was coming round to Dr Knight's flat when I saw him on the pavement. I was rather surprised to find him…unsupervised.'

'That was entirely my fault,' Jonathan said. 'I thought I had made that clear.'

'Miss Richardson is responsible for you when you're in her care,' Derrick snapped, 'under all circumstances.'

'But I trust you're not going to blame her for my foolishness?'

Tania could see that Jonathan was about to lose his temper. Fortunately, Derrick saw it, too. 'Of course not,' he said smoothly. 'These things happen. Now, could you escort Dr Knight back to your car, please, Miss Richardson, and then if we could have a quick word in private?'

'I'll be right with you,' she said.

But Jonathan had a word in private first. 'If that man tries to tell you off for what I did, I want to know,' he said thinly. 'I just won't have it.'

'You've caused me enough trouble without getting me into more. I can fight my own battles. This time, stay in the car!'

She walked back to Derrick. Whatever he had to say to her, secretly she felt she deserved it. She had been in charge of Jonathan. But what he asked her left her startled and a little bit afraid.

'Are you enamoured of this man?' he asked.

Enamoured? *Enamoured?* Only Derrick could use a word like that. But what was she to answer? She had to pause. 'Well...I do like him a lot,' she said. 'He's good company.'

'You're not being paid to enjoy his company!' Derrick's voice deepened, took on a sonorous tone she had heard before when he was asking for extra funding at a Board of Trustees meeting. 'Remember, we don't sign the Hippocratic oath, but I do feel we have a duty to our clients—our patients. We cannot take advantage of them! Dr Knight has just suffered a traumatic experience, he's vulnerable. You know what this feeling for you is—it's transference. Dr Knight has no regard for you as a person, just for you as a helper. You're doing wrong to yourself—and to him—if you think any regard could grow. Do I make myself clear?'

She had to fight back somehow. 'Perfectly clear,' she said crisply. 'Mr Gee, you can rest assured that I will act entirely professionally. And now I think I'd better get back to my client.'

Angrily she walked back to the car. Never, never again would she give Derrick cause to speak to her like that!

'Am I in disgrace?' Jonathan asked as she climbed into the car, viciously twisted the ignition key. 'Because if I am, I'm sorry.'

'You don't sound very sorry. No, you're not in disgrace.'

'But you are. I won't have it, Tania.'

'There's nothing you can do about it. He's my boss. Would you let one of your patients tell you how to deal with one of your staff?'

'Probably not,' he said reflectively, 'but I like to think I'd listen first. Now, judging by the jerky way you're driving this car, he said something to upset you. I want to know what it was.'

'You can't always have what you want! And I'm driving this car perfectly well! And how do you know it concerns you?'

'You'd drive a lot better if you got things off your chest. Sharing a trouble halves it. And all the things your mother used to say to you. I know it's about me and you're going to have to tell me what he said. Tania, I feel responsible.'

'All right, I'll think about it. But not in the car. And you have to promise—here and now and honestly— that you won't lose your temper.'

'If I'm angry I lose my temper,' he shouted. 'That's the way people are!'

'Well, change!' she shouted back. 'And don't think you're the only person in the world with a temper.'

There was silence for a few minutes. She was seething with rage and for a moment she wondered why. Then she realised. Derrick had been too perceptive. He had seen a relationship between her and Jonathan that she hadn't been fully aware of herself. That worried her.

Jonathan said in a perfectly calm voice, 'I promise to keep my temper. We'll go back to the flat, I'll make you a coffee and then you can tell me what he said.'

'All right,' she said, equally calmly. Only then did she start to worry. Did she have to tell him that she'd owned up to having a...regard for him?

*   *   *

They sat by the window, the blinds pulled to filter the sun's rays. Tania sipped her coffee and wondered what exactly she could say. Jonathan was calm now, giving her time to organise her thoughts, to prepare. That made things worse.

Eventually she had to speak. She swallowed, her throat suddenly dry. This was hard! 'Derrick reminded me that though we don't have to sign the Hippocratic oath, we are in a sense carers like doctors or nurses. We have a responsibility to our clients—our patients, if you like.'

'And which clause of the Hippocratic oath did you break?'

'I didn't! But Derrick thought…Derrick suggested…the bit about having a relationship with your patient.' She was stronger now she had said it. 'He asked if I was enamoured of you, pointed out that you were very vulnerable at the moment.'

Jonathan brooded. 'He's quite right, of course,' he said eventually. 'I could be vulnerable. Sexual relationships between a carer and a patient are always problematical. He was only doing his job.'

'I'm glad you think so,' she said, not able to hide her dismay.

'Remember, I said problematical, not wrong. What did you say when he asked you if you were enamoured of me?' He snorted, 'And enamoured is a wonderful word. But what did you say?'

'I said…I think I said…that I liked you a lot.'

'Well, thank you. This isn't the time for exchanging compliments, but I like you a lot, too. Now, Tania, was Derrick upset about our relationship because he thought it was wrong? Or because he has designs on you him-self?'

'Derrick?' Designs on me? That's another quaint ex-pression, isn't it?' She tried to be light-hearted but it didn't work.

'Don't try to avoid the question! And don't try to lie to me, I'll be able to tell. Have you ever been out with him? Has he ever asked you out?'

'You're beginning to shout,' she accused, 'and you don't have to, you know. A temper is quite easy to control and losing it gets you nowhere.'

'I've found that having a temper is useful sometimes. People accept too much. If you're right, you should say so and stick by it.'

'If you're right,' she shot back at him. 'But if you're wrong, you just look a fool.'

'A risk that I'm willing to take.' He also drank some coffee. 'I know we like each other quite a lot, Tania. But are you actually enamoured of me?'

'We'll end this conversation right now,' she said.

'Not quite yet. I think…it's possible…that *I* might be enamoured of *you*.'

After that Tania took Jonathan into the garden in the front of the flats and they practised walking round the gravel paths. There were no cars here and the few peo-ple they met were neighbours who introduced them-selves and commiserated. Tania thought it was an ideal place for him to practise—in time he would be able to come out here on his own.

'I've had clients whose front door opened straight onto a busy main road,' she told him. 'There's just nowhere for them to practise.'

'I guess I'm lucky in some things,' he told her. 'If I start grumbling, remind me.'

'I will,' she said.

She stayed with him longer than perhaps she ought. But it was her own time, and she could do with it what she wanted. None of her other clients was suffering, her bookwork was all complete. Finally, when she said it was time to go and had taken him back to his flat, he asked her to sit down a minute. 'I've something to ask you,' he said. 'It's a bit of a problem.'

Practically for the first time since she had met him, Jonathan seemed uncomfortable. Usually he was quite at his ease, happy in any social situation. But not now. He seemed at a loss for words, not sure what to say.

'Not like you,' she teased. 'I thought problems were things that other people had.'

'So did I. But there's something new every day.' He scowled. 'I want to invite you somewhere. Tonight. But I don't know if you're doing anything. And I don't know whether to ask you as a woman or as a professional carer whom I can pay for doing extra work with me.'

She hadn't expected this! 'Well, I've got no plans for tonight,' she said. 'And I've never done extra work for money, though I've no objection to it. I know some of my colleagues do. In fact, I have done odd bits extra here and there, but because I wanted to. That's all.'

He remained silent. Tania took a deep breath. She knew she was chancing something, this was probably not a good idea. She had only to say no and their relationship could continue as before. She liked Jonathan. Did she want to chance things changing between them? Because after this things would never be the same again, and the thought frightened her. This was a massive step into the unknown. She didn't do things like this.

But… 'Ask me as a woman,' she said. It was done.

'I used to go out to dinner a lot,' he said. 'Often I'd take someone, perhaps a lady like yourself. And I liked to be…in charge.'

She grinned at him, knowing that her feelings would come out in her voice. 'And now you can't,' she mocked gently. 'Jonathan, this is going to be very good for you. A lesson in humility. Where are you going to take me?'

'The Blue Bell,' he said. 'It's a pub I go to a lot.'

'No, it isn't,' she contradicted. 'I've never been but I've heard of it. It's a very posh restaurant with a bar attached. It's been written up in the Sunday papers. They wouldn't like you calling it a pub. But are you sure you ought to go there while you're—?'

His face set. 'It's a place I go to,' he said. 'I'm not going to stop doing things that I used to just be-cause…because of some small difficulty.'

'Fine,' she said gently, 'I entirely agree. But there's one condition. I'm still your rehabilitation worker. If I say something is necessary, you don't argue.'

'Agreed. Meet at half past seven, dinner at eight? I'll phone and book a table.'

'That'll be lovely. I'll call for you here at—'

'No.' Jonathan's voice was courteous but deter-mined. 'I'm taking you out. We'll take a taxi, I have an account with a local firm. It'll be no problem to anyone. I'll pick you up.'

Things were going too fast now. She had climbed onto a roller-coaster and there was no way of stopping it. 'All right,' she said, 'you can pick me up. I live at the school, you know, in one of the nurses' rooms. If you arrive outside the foyer at about half past seven…I'll be there.'

'You don't want me to pick you up at your room?'

'Well, it'd be difficult to give you instructions on how to get there with a long cane,' she said.

Tania decided to check her desk when she got back to the school. There was a note there from Derrick to ring him on his mobile.

She sighed. She'd had enough of Derrick for one day. If it was about Jonathan or any of her other clients, then fine. He was entitled to get in touch. But she suspected that wasn't the case. She reached for the phone.

'Tania! Good to hear from you. I thought we parted a bit at cross-purposes this afternoon, but that's all behind us now. I'm sorry if I seemed a little angry and I want to make things up. It's just because I'm concerned about you.'

'No need to worry, Derrick. I'm fine.' She hoped the cold tone would be enough to signal what she thought. It wasn't.

'Glad to hear it. But I think we ought to, well, show that we're working well together. What about a drink tonight at about nine? I could pick you up, we could drive out into the country somewhere.'

She knew it wasn't just a drink he wanted. He'd forgotten what she'd told him about people having relationships at work. 'Sorry, Derrick, I can't. In fact, I'm already going out tonight.'

His voice was sharp. 'I didn't know you were seeing anybody. I do hope it's not that Dr Knight. I've warned you about him, Tania. Who are you going out with?'

She didn't want to but she had to make her position clear. 'That's my business. And I thought I'd made it clear to you—I think relationships at work are always a bad idea. I'd never go out with a man I worked for.'

Now he was angry. 'I think you should remember what I've done for you, Tania! You're only a temporary employee at present. And I arranged the room in the nurses' home!'

'So you think I've got to pay you back? Too bad!' She slammed down the phone. The cheek of the man!

She thought she would be in a bad temper, expected to be upset. But very quickly she forgot Derrick and started to enjoy herself. She hadn't been out with a man for months, she calculated. Men always meant trouble to her, and if she did go out, it wasn't with a man like Jonathan. But she was going out tonight, in a couple of hours, and she intended to enjoy herself. She had a long bath and picked out a dress she hadn't had occasion to wear for some time. A girl along the corridor had been a hairdresser before she'd trained to be a nurse, and she blow-dried and pinned up Tania's long hair.

She was ready by seven—half an hour to go. Apprehensive now, Tania sat on her bed. This was the best-looking man she had ever been out with, the most dynamic and the... It's not the same, she told herself. For a start, he couldn't see her. And yet she knew, despite what Derrick had said, that he wasn't vulnerable. If anyone was, she was.

She walked out of the foyer and was waiting and watching on the edge of the kerb when the taxi arrived. It wasn't the usual cheap and cheerful taxi firm that she used, with the telephone number stuck to the side. Instead, it was a large black car, with only the driver in a black suit to show it was for hire. The driver got out and opened the back door for her.

They set off and she turned to see Jonathan scowling. 'Normally I'd open the door for you myself,' he said, 'but I was afraid of tripping over something.'

'A wise decision on your part,' she said cheerfully. 'I wouldn't want you to stain that suit. I must say, you look very nice.'

He was wearing a very light grey suit in some soft material she didn't recognise but suspected was expensive. His shirt was a light blue, his tie a darker blue silk.

'I got Joe to give me a hand to get dressed,' he confessed. 'Don't forget, I run—used to run a department. Learning how to delegate is all-important. But now…' He reached behind him and offered her a box. 'I didn't know what colour dress you'd be wearing so I chose white. It goes with most things.'

She accepted the little Cellophane box and gasped. Inside was an orchid—pure white in colour. 'I'm wearing a blue dress,' she said, 'and this will go wonderfully with it. May I pin it on now?'

'I hoped you would. Now, you know I love feminine beauty, and I know you'll have made an effort, even though I can't see you. So I want you to describe your dress.'

'Well, right now I think I look very nice.' Tania described the dress, let him run his hand across her shoulder to feel the material, touch her hair to have some idea of the style she had picked.

'And I recognise your perfume,' he said, and named it.

She looked at him, amazed. 'You have a very good nose,' she said. 'Not one man in a thousand would have recognised that.'

'Learned at my mother's knee,' he said smugly. 'I like perfumes.'

They sat silently for a few minutes. She was considering something, wondering exactly how to say it. After a while he said, 'Tania, I can almost hear you thinking. You have a problem and I want to know what it is.'

She was shocked. 'You're right! But how did you know?'

'We're sitting next to each other. I can tell that you're uncomfortable. You keep changing position and your breathing is faster than normal.' He paused a moment, then said, 'Being blind does make your other senses more acute.'

'I see. All right, I'll tell you what it is. I've changed my mind. You asked me out tonight as a woman, largely because I told you to. Now I think things ought to be different. It would be better if you paid me for my time.'

'As you wish,' he said placidly. 'I have no problem with that. But will you tell me why? Not suddenly had the brokers in, I trust?'

'You're making fun of me! No, this is a matter of…principle really. A small principle. I think you're good to the women you take out. You think about them, worry about them. Now you're taking me out, but when eventually you see me you might be disappointed. This way, you won't need to feel too badly when you drop me. Our relationship will have been purely a professional one.'

Jonathan took her hand. 'You worry too much about things,' he said. 'I'm not going to talk about what you've just said, except to say wait and see. Now enjoy yourself.'

As he spoke the car drew up outside the front door of the Blue Bell. The driver came to open the door, she offered Jonathan her arm and whispered what was in front of them. 'About five paces and then a step up. There's a man with shiny black hair and a dark suit come to look at us. He seems worried.'

'Albert. The *maître d'*. I spoke to him earlier.'

Albert glided forward. 'Dr Knight, how good to see you! But in such unfortunate circumstances. May I say you have the good wishes of myself and the staff here. We will do all we can to be of assistance.'

'Hello, Albert. This is Miss Richardson.'

Albert turned to her. 'Miss Richardson, welcome to the Blue Bell. I don't think you've been here before. I trust you will enjoy our meal and visit us again.'

Somehow they were eased inside and seated at a table near the bar. Tania thought Jonathan was doing very well. With his hand on her arm it looked as if he were guiding her, not the other way round.

'A drink, Miss Richardson?' Albert queried. 'Dr Knight, your usual sherry?'

'Please, Albert. Tania, unless you have your mind set on something else, may I suggest you have a sherry, too? It's Albert's special bottle.'

'A sherry will be fine,' she muttered, and Albert was gone.

'Do you like it here?' Jonathan asked. 'We'll have a drink and then when you're ready Albert will come to take our order. And then he'll take us to the table when the meal is ready.'

'It's not like a shandy, pie and chips at my local,' she said, 'but I like it very much.'

The anteroom they were in was half-full. Apparently everyone sat here for a drink before going into the main dining room. It was cool, there was an unobtrusive air-conditioning system. The chairs were comfortable, in dark red leather that matched the carpet. There was the soft hum of conversation, the odd peal of laughter. Tania looked at the other guests. The older lady on her left—surely those earrings couldn't be real diamonds? But her dress was expensive enough. And she could see out into the car park. There was a Bentley and a couple of Jaguars. Quite a place.

Their sherries came. Then a young waitress came round and gave them a small plate each, and put half a dozen tiny pastries on each. They were warm and smelt delicious. 'I'd come here just for these *bonne-bouches*,' Jonathan said. 'Try one, Tania.'

She did. The thinnest of crisp pasty crusts with a centre of a prawn in sauce. Just a mouthful, but wonderful. 'Very nice indeed,' she said. 'I'm enjoying myself.'

Shortly afterwards Albert came to discuss the menu. 'I've already had a word with him myself,' Jonathan said. 'We've worked out a meal that I can eat without too much trouble.'

'Good,' she said. She knew how mortified newly blind people could feel when they realised how difficult it could be to eat some things. Sauces could be a particular problem. So were peas.

She took Albert's and Jonathan's advice when selecting her meal: a terrine of fish with apple chutney; roast chump of lamb with onion marmalade and rosemarie jus; apple galette with butterscotch sauce. And all the trimmings, of course. Albert and Jonathan discussed the wines and she left them to it.

'Is there anything else you want?' Jonathan asked finally. 'Any way Albert can make our meal more special?'

She hesitated. There was something, and he caught

her hesitation. 'Tell us,' he said softly. 'We can't guess.'

Well, she was really looking forward to this meal and there was something that would spoil it for her. Spoil it slightly. 'Could we have a table without candles, please?' she asked.

'Of course, madam,' Albert said, and that was settled. He left.

'Candles are supposed to be romantic,' Jonathan said. 'They create an atmosphere. But I suppose you have to remind us that we're still patient and carer?'

'This will keep things a bit professional. And anyway, I can be romantic enough without candles.' Then she realised what she had just said. 'Oh, dear! I didn't mean—'

'I know what you meant,' he said. 'Now, before we dine, I think I owe you this.' From his pocket he took a wallet, the notes in it carefully arranged in the way she had shown him. He took some out and offered them to her. 'I'm blind,' he said. 'It's no good sending me a bill.'

She had said it, but when it came to actually accepting money she knew she couldn't do it. 'I can't take it,' she said. 'I just can't take it. I'm having a wonderful time, I'm enjoying myself. You know I said it for a reason but…' Her voice rose to a squeak. 'Any anyway, not that much!'

'If you take it, I can ask you out again,' Jonathan said. 'Tell you what, let's compromise. Take the money and buy something for your blind school. Or give it to one of the charities there.'

Very reluctantly Tania took what he had offered her. 'I'll give it to the guide-dog fund,' she said. 'It'll be money well spent.'

'Good. Now, we can talk about something else. Do you know, every conversation we've had has been about me? Well, I want to change that. I want to talk about you.'

Instantly she was cautious. Jonathan might be blind but he was one of the shrewdest people she had ever met. She didn't want to talk about herself—she would reveal more than she wished. 'I'm not a very interesting person,' she said.

'You interest me. Why has such an attractive, such an intelligent, such a pleasant person not been snapped up? I know that's a presumption—but there's something about you that suggests you're not looking for a relationship.'

'Thank you for the compliment,' she said tartly. 'Don't forget, it's not everyone's ambition to be in a relationship. In fact, I've just turned down an offer—I think.'

'Don't tell me—Derrick. I thought there was something rather…proprietorial about his attitude to you.'

'Derrick sometimes gets things wrong. But he hasn't been a bad boss. What do you want to know about me?'

'Everything,' he said flatly.

Tania tried to drag her thoughts together. What should she tell him, and what not? She couldn't show all of herself to this man. 'Well…I'm twenty-seven years old and I'm an only child. I was brought up by my mother, my father died when I was young. But my mother and I, we got on well together.'

'We have that in common,' he said.

'Yes, well… I was training to be a nurse. In fact, I did two years. I loved it. Jonathan, I'm not sure I want to tell you this. Anyway, it's all boring.'

'You could never bore me,' he said gently, 'and certainly if you don't want to talk there's no need to. If it causes you pain, you're under no pressure. But I want to know you better, Tania. And I think you're hiding something. It could be good for you to talk. To trust someone.'

'I trusted someone before!' she said bitterly. 'Sorry, please, forget I said that.'

'And there's another story,' he said reflectively. 'But, first, what about your mother?'

It was odd telling this to someone who was blind. She could stare into Jonathan's face, see how it hardened into anger, softened into sympathy. She'd never done this before.

'I was a dedicated nurse,' she said. 'I worked like mad, passed all the examinations, got commendations and so on—and I enjoyed the work itself. But during this time my mother's sight was deteriorating. She had cataracts, we were waiting till they were ripe. I knew this but I thought she was coping. I spent a lot of time at home. But not enough. Perhaps I didn't notice because I didn't want to notice. Anyway, my mother went out, tried to cross the road and got run down. I was at the hospital when they told me.'

The horror of that day had never left her.

'You don't have to go on if you don't want to,' Jonathan said softly.

'No, I...I'd like you to know the whole story. My mother was paralysed. A tetraplegic. She wanted me to put her in a home but I wouldn't. For four years I looked after her, and then she died. I couldn't face starting to nurse again—and I heard of this course for blind rehabilitation workers in Harrogate. I did it and have enjoyed my work ever since.'

He reached over, found her hands and stroked them. 'A sobering story,' he said. 'You sacrificed your—'

'I sacrificed nothing!' she snapped. 'I only did what I wanted and I was so happy with my mother. I wanted to—'

'Your table is ready,' Albert said, suddenly materialising by their side. 'If you are ready now…'

He led them to a table in a little alcove, taking care, Tania noticed, to lead them where there was no chance of Jonathan tripping on anything. When they were seated he saw that glasses were to hand, that Jonathan could reach anything he needed. Then the wine was opened and their first courses brought.

The wine and her terrine with apple chutney were both delightful. Neither of them said anything during the first course, it was sufficient to eat. The second course was, if anything, even better. But when the plates were removed, they decided to wait a while before dessert. It would be something to look forward to.

Jonathan poured more wine and asked, 'So did you feel guilty about your mother's accident? Did you move into this kind of work as some kind of recompense?'

'Possibly. I know there was no need to feel guilty— a hundred people have told me that. But people can't tell you how to feel.'

'That I know well. But I suspect—'

'Enough about me,' she said. 'I'm really enjoying being with you, and the meal is fantastic, so I don't want to drag over old miseries. Now I want to know about you. Why aren't you married?'

He realised that she wanted to change the mood and went along with her unspoken wishes. 'Well, I'm a doctor, a consultant in infectious diseases. It's not a glamorous branch of medicine, but I like it. So far in my life I've worked hard at medicine and been frivolous in the rest of my life. I love beautiful women. Their hair, their faces, their skin, their bodies. Women of any age. My mother is beautiful. It's not sexual—I just like beauty.'

Tania felt rather upset. 'That's a bit frivolous,' she said. 'Their beauty isn't much of a way of judging someone's worth. There are lots of other ways…beauty shouldn't be important.'

'True. I think an awful lot of you, Tania, but the fact that you're beautiful is a definite extra.'

'How do you know I'm beautiful?' she said. 'You've never even seen me!'

'Joe told me,' he said flatly. 'We're very close, I trust his judgement. And the judgement of others. I'm fighting this blindness, trying to accept it. But you should know, one of the reasons I want to regain my sight is to see you.'

She sighed. 'Jonathan, you've had a terrible, traumatic experience, you're upset. You're not yourself, you shouldn't make statements like that, you might come to regret them.'

'Are you sure I don't mean them?'

She knew she had to give him an honest answer. And it wasn't in her to lie. 'No,' she said, her lips dry, 'I think you probably do mean what you say. Now, can we, please, forget me completely?'

'All right. I'll get our dessert served, shall I?' It was something else she liked about him. He knew when to stop pushing.

After their meal they went back to the bar again and had coffee and liqueurs. 'I'm really enjoying myself tonight,' he said, 'and it's nothing to do with you, but I didn't expect to.'

She was surprised. 'If you didn't expect to enjoy yourself, why did you come?'

'I had to prove to myself that there were parts of my old life I could still cope with. And being with you gives me confidence. Not many people do, you know— but you do.'

'I'm glad,' she said simply.

'So-o, since you've been working for me part time— and since we've both enjoyed it—would you like to work for me again?'

She laughed. 'If this is work, then I want overtime. What have you in mind?'

There's a hospital ball two weeks Saturday. Black tie, dancing, lots of people to meet. Basically it's a charity function, we thank people who have given to the hospital. I want to go so that people can see that I'm still on top of things. I might have had an accident, but I'm still the consultant.'

'Is that so important to you?'

'It may be a character flaw but, yes, it is. I'm sorry.'

'It's the first time I've heard you admit to having a flaw,' she said. 'I think it needs recognising. All right, I'd love to come with you.'

His face lit up. 'You'll be the belle of the ball,' he said. 'And everyone will be jealous of me.'

'That's enough! I want to talk about something else now. We've been serious long enough.'

When it was time, Jonathan phoned for the car. On the way back to the school he said, 'You were waiting at the edge of the pavement when we picked you up. Tell me how you get from there to the foyer.'

'It's no distance. There's a concrete path that runs round the corner of the main block and straight to the door.'

'The corner? Is that a right angle? And can you feel the edge of the path with a long cane?'

Tania realised why he was asking. 'You want to escort me to the front door,' she said. 'Jonathan, I'll be fine. If you want, the driver can come with me, but there's no need.'

'Never in my life have I left a lady to walk back to her front door and I'm not going to start now. From what you say I should be able to navigate there and back with my cane. So I will.'

She realised how important it was to him. 'All right,' she said, 'I'd really like that. Just one thing. I'm going to wait by the door until I hear the car drive away. Then I'll know you're safe, too.'

'I can live with that,' he said.

She didn't guide him. She let him tap his way along the edge of the path, negotiate the corner, take her to the glassed-in entrance. He held her arm but she gave him no help. And then they were at the door. 'You did well,' she said.

'It was only an excuse. I wanted to be alone with you.' And his arms wrapped round her.

It was only a tentative kiss at first. His mouth found hers, touched gently, his hold on her light. She realised this was what she had been expecting, what she had been wanting. There was a moment's apprehension, a wondering if she was doing the right thing. She'd done nothing like this for so long!

But it was wonderful! She clutched him to her, pressed her body to his, offering herself because she wanted to. And he responded. She felt his hold on her tighten, their bodies seemed to cling together as if they were naked. His tongue probed deep into her, she was carried away on waves of sensation she had never experienced before. What was the man doing to her or, rather, what was she doing to herself?

She wanted to stay here, like this, for ever. But something deep inside her said that it shouldn't go on too long. So far it had been only a goodnight kiss. It mustn't be allowed to turn into anything more. There were good reasons.

She broke off their kiss, put her hands on his chest. 'I must go now,' she murmured. 'Thank you, Jonathan, I've had a marvellous evening.'

He ignored her trite little words. 'You know things will never be the same between us again,' he demanded. 'That was more than a kiss. It was a declaration.'

She moved uneasily. 'Perhaps so,' she admitted. 'But for the moment—until you have things settled—we must take things slowly.'

'You mean, wait until we know if I'm blind or not?' he said bluntly.

'Yes. I wouldn't have put it as cruelly as that but, yes, I won't change how I feel—but you very well might.'

For a moment Tania thought he would argue. But then he kissed her on the cheek and stepped away from her. 'Goodnight, sweetheart. I can't remember a night I've enjoyed more—either with my sight or without it.'

Jonathan turned, reached out with his long cane and tapped the side of the path. She watched him make his slow progress, pause at the bend and then turn the corner. He was out of sight. She didn't move. A little later there was the sound of a car being driven away. He had reached the taxi safely. Then she went in to her room.

It was only a room, small, with institutional furniture, but it was her home. She had added her own touches—pictures on the walls, a pretty throw on the bed, a mobile that she had seen and thought was fun. But now it was the last place she wanted to be.

She undressed, slipped on a light dressing-gown, hung up her clothes. Then she sat on the bed and thought about her evening, starting with the kiss and then moving backwards. She had enjoyed herself so much. The meal had been fantastic, the surroundings equally so, but most of all she had enjoyed Jonathan's company. It felt so good to be escorted by such a handsome man.

She had answered his questions with an honesty that she hadn't shown to any man for years. She was happy that he knew about her mother. But as she sat there, her smile slowly disappeared. She had another secret that nothing would make her tell. Unconsciously, her hand slid inside her gown, her fingertips stroking the naked flesh of her abdomen.

The memory didn't come back so often now. There had been times when she would wake in the middle of the night, bathed in sweat, terrified by a nightmare that had its origin in months of pain in hospital.

The memories came to her again, and she knew she couldn't just ignore them. She would have to follow them to the bitter end.

It had happened in her home, when her spirits were at their lowest, just after her mother had died. A silly, a pointless accident. She had tripped over a rug in the living room, fallen and hit her head on the corner of the mantelpiece. She had been knocked unconscious.

Serious enough, but there had been more. It had been winter and she had brought in a small electric fire to warm the room. An old electric fire, with a naked element.

She had fallen across the fire, landed waist down on it. The element had burned through her dress to her flesh. It had also set fire to the newspaper she'd been holding.

She had been unconscious, and burning.

A neighbour had seen the flames through the window, had kicked in the door, dragged her away and then sent for an ambulance. She'd woken up in the specialist burns unit, having suffered third-degree burns.

Behind her wardrobe door there was a full-length mirror, usually this door was kept closed. Now she opened it fully and slipped off her gown. She surveyed herself, naked, in the mirror.

Jonathan had said that he loved beautiful women. He loved their faces, hair, bodies, skin. Well, yes, she was beautiful. She wasn't being arrogant, it was a fair and detached assessment. Her breasts were high and full, her waist slim, her hips rounded and her legs long. But in between all these was a mass of scar tissue. Her abdomen showed great weals, inflamed skin, the marks of unsuccessful plastic surgery.

She burst into tears. No lover of beautiful women could ever look at her and be anything but repulsed.

CHAPTER FIVE

FIRST thing next morning Tania walked to her office. There were a couple of hours' paperwork at her desk before she could start on her calls. A note on her desk asked her to bring the files on Dr Knight and one or two others of her clients to Derrick's office.

There was no reference to yesterday's conversation. He was curt but businesslike, what he had to say was soon over. But then he followed it with 'Did you enjoy yourself at the Blue Bell last night?'

She just wasn't expecting this. 'Yes, I did, very much,' she said, 'but how did you know?'

'I was told this morning by the head of this school. He called in there for a drink. He seemed to think it quite funny to see you there, with a client.' Derrick paused for effect. 'I don't think it's funny at all. I feel I should have been informed in advance.'

'What I do in my own time is my own business,' she said defiantly.

'Quite so.' He took up her report on her work with Jonathan, looked through it. 'However, I feel that your conduct with Dr Knight hasn't been entirely professional. I don't intend to pursue this—but I do intend to remove him from your care. I think it better for our client if someone else is his rehabilitation worker.'

She looked at Derrick in horror. 'You can't do this! You're only moving me because I wouldn't go out with you. It's mean, nasty and spiteful.'

'First of all, I can do it. I can move any of my workers for whatever reason I think fit. Secondly, in no way am I doing this because of anything…personal between us. And any tribunal you care to complain to would agree with me.'

'Well, I want at least to say goodbye—'

'No! And that, Miss Richardson, is a specific instruction. You are not to get in touch with Dr Knight. Stay in the office this morning. I see you were intending to visit. I'm sending April Manson in your place.'

'April Manson?' Tania said incredulously. 'You're not sending April Manson?'

She knew that Jonathan and April just wouldn't get on. April was a big booming woman, who only got on well with people who didn't mind her bossy nature. With some clients it was an approach that worked. It wouldn't work with Jonathan.

'April is an experienced and able worker. Good morning, Miss Richardson.'

She walked out of his office in a daze. This was the last thing she had expected. Slumping at her desk, she wondered about her future. Perhaps it was time she moved on. Now she would never be able to work comfortably with Derrick. And her position was precarious—she was only a temporary worker after all, could be sacked at a moment's notice. And what about Jonathan? She would phone him tonight. On her own time.

There was more paperwork to get on with. She supposed that compiling statistical returns was necessary and might even be useful—to somebody. It took her mind off things, but it was dreary.

After an hour she lifted her head, hearing sounds of argument outside. This wasn't uncommon. Often the boarders had loud arguments about something or other. But this seemed different.

Suddenly, behind her, her office door crashed open. A voice she recognised shouted, loudly, angrily, 'Tania…Tania…where are you?'

She turned her head in horror. There in the doorway was Jonathan—dressed in his customary T-shirt and chinos. And judging by his face, he was angry! He was holding—or being held by—April Manson. For the first time ever April seemed to be out of control of a situation. She looked red-faced and anxious.

'Jonathan? What are you doing here? You shouldn't be—'

'I've come to see you and to see you boss, Gee. Incidentally, I would at least have expected a phone call from you, Tania. But the way this place is run…'

She knew it would cause trouble. But for the moment she just didn't care. Seeing Jonathan had made her feel happy and reckless, in equal proportions. 'I was specifically ordered not to phone you,' she said. 'But I would have called tonight.'

'I see.' Jonathan turned to the quaking April and said, 'Thank you for your help, Miss Manson, but now Miss Richardson will be taking over. I don't need you any more.'

'But Mr Gee said—'

'What Mr Gee said will be unsaid. Now, goodbye!' April hesitated a moment, then scuttled away.

'Tania, will you, please, come and take me to Mr Gee's office?'

She went over, put his hand on her arm. 'I can take you over there, Jonathan. But do you think it's wise? Why not phone for an appointment?'

'I made another appointment for this morning. With

you. It wasn't kept. Now I'm going to find out why. So let's go to see this Mr Gee.'

'Well, his secretary is outside so we could ask her—'

'No. We walk past and tell her where we're going. Now, take me to his room!'

She could have argued, of course. But an angry Jonathan was a fearsome sight. Ann, Derrick's secretary, looked up from her computer as Tania led Jonathan into her little outer room. 'I'm afraid Mr Gee's rather busy at the moment, Tania,' she said. 'I think—'

'Busy or not, we're going in to see him,' Jonathan said. 'There's no need to announce us, we'll announce ourselves.'

'But Tania…Mr…you can't…'

Jonathan pushed Tania forwards. She had no option but to ignore Ann's plaintive call and lead him to the door of Derrick's office. Wondering just where this all would end, she opened the door.

Derrick looked up, half alarmed, half puzzled. 'Tania? Dr Knight? I'm sorry but I just don't have time at the moment to—'

'You will find time,' Jonathan roared, 'and you'll find time right now!' In a quieter voice he added, 'Tania, please find me a chair and put it facing Mr Gee's desk.'

She did so, then led him to it. At the same time Derrick was saying, 'this is most unprofessional. There is a system if you wish to speak to me, a means whereby I—'

Now Jonathan was comfortable. He leaned forward, touched the edge of Derrick's desk and snarled, 'I believe that my case and my treatment were discussed in this office this morning. I was neither consulted nor informed. No attempt was made to canvass my views. I may be blind but I still have the rest of my faculties. This was a piece of gross impertinence and, to use your own word, was most unprofessional. What have you to say?'

Derrick looked wildly around his office. Something like this had never happened to him before, and he quite obviously didn't know what to do. 'Dr Knight, we often discuss our clients and consider future treatments. In this case I thought—'

'I very much doubt that you thought! If you had thought, you would have asked me. I'm a health professional myself, Mr Gee, and I'm capable of commenting on my own treatment. I believe that by removing Miss Richardson you have significantly affected my therapy. This is in no way a comment on Miss Manson, who, I'm sure, is very competent, but Miss Richardson here and myself have established a very good working relationship.'

'Relationship!' Derrick seized on the word. Obviously he thought that this might give him a chance to fight back. 'I was concerned with the growing relationship between yourself and your rehabilitation worker. I thought it undesirable.'

'Undesirable to me or to yourself? You acted because of purely personal reasons, Mr Gee—because of your own feelings for Miss Richardson. Now, does my care revert to Miss Richardson or do I have to make a formal complaint? And when I say complaint, I'm talking about referring your conduct to the Board of Trustees of this place, also instructing my solicitor to make a claim for damages from your good self.'

There was an appalled silence. Then Jonathan said quietly, 'Of course, this all may have been a misunderstanding. No more need be said if things revert to how they were. If you need to speak to us, Miss Richardson and myself will be in the garden. Tania?'

She looked at Derrick. She had never seen a man so stricken. He just nodded. She led Jonathan into the garden, where they sat together on a bench in the sun.

'I didn't lose my temper,' he protested. 'Didn't you hear me speak quite calmly to him just before we left?'

'You weren't speaking calmly! You were doing what my mother called shouting quietly. You were dreadful.'

'Perhaps,' he said, 'but that man's a bully, and I detest bullies. And to send that April Manson in your place! That was sheer cruelty, sheer vindictiveness. She might be competent at her job, but the woman has the sensitivity of a blunt chisel. Asked if I wouldn't like floral curtains for the big window?'

Tania giggled. 'In her way April is very good,' she said. 'A lot of our clients like her.'

'Those with pink net curtains. Now, tell me exactly what did happen this morning.'

Tania thought. 'Well, in spite of what you shouted at him,' she said, 'he did have a point. He knew we'd been getting…involved and that kind of thing can harm both the reputation of this school and the welfare of our clients. And we are warned to watch out for clients who want to get emotionally involved with us.'

'And was that the only reason for moving you? Tell me honestly.'

She knew he would detect it if she was telling a lie. 'No,' she said. 'He found out we'd been out together last night and he didn't like it.'

'Fair enough. Now, where are we up to in my training?'

*   *   *

Tania was glad to be allowed to carry on working with Jonathan. A message had been sent out to them—not from Derrick in person—that for the moment it would be all right for Miss Richardson to continue with Dr Knight's rehabilitation. So she had brought him back to his flat and was now concentrating on further long-stick work around the gardens of the flats. After a while she said, 'I'm going up to the flat to fetch us both a glass of orange. You're on your own now, Jonathan. But stay in the garden!'

'I will,' he said. In many ways it was an ideal place to work. There was no traffic. The paths were gravel, not concrete, so there was no edge for him to feel, but he could tell the difference between the softness of the grass and the crunchy gravel.

In the middle of the garden was a concrete square, with a pool and a fountain in its centre. She left him learning how to walk round the pool and then make for a wooden bench. He was quick to learn and it was heartening to watch him.

When Tania came back he was as absorbed as ever, practising moves over and over again. She told him to find a bench and they would sit down for a while. He wasn't to work too hard.

'I enjoyed last night so much,' he said. 'I've been replaying it in my memory. And I was so much looking forward to seeing you this morning—that is, to you coming—and then that woman turned up!'

'Well, I'm here now,' she said placidly, 'and I enjoyed last night very much as well.'

'Good. Now, tell me about the candles.'

She couldn't help it. She knew she flinched and she knew he'd noticed it. 'All forms of naked flame are a danger to those with impaired vision,' she said. 'I don't like open fires either.'

'Hmm. I thought there might be a more personal reason to your dislike.' Jonathan was as astute as ever. 'Well, I once did have an accident,' she told him, 'but, please, don't ask me about it. I don't like to talk about it.'

'Some time perhaps? I want to know all about you, Tania.'

'All right, some time I might. Now, let's talk about you. When I looked down at you from the flat while you were working there seemed to be an intensity about what you were doing. You were concentrating far more than the job needed. The sun's shining. You should be enjoying yourself.'

'I was just trying to learn,' he said.

'No, you weren't. You're a friend, Jonathan, and friends confide in each other. You're working too hard at keeping a stiff upper lip, you're bottling up what you're feeling. It's not good for you.'

'I don't fancy whining about what can't be changed to other people. It's my problem, mine alone. I'll cope my way.'

Gently, she said, 'Jonathan, you're not alone, it's good to share. I can tell you're feeling a bit low. Please, tell me why.'

It was warm there in the garden, and there was the scent of flowers and newly mown grass. She moved her hand to touch his arm, the skin was warm. He clutched her hand, pressed it to him. He said, the words slow and faltering, 'Well, I suppose I'm like everyone else in this predicament. Every now and again—in my case it's often the early morning—it hits me. I might be blind for the rest of my life. And I'm…' His voice tailed away.

'It'll help if you say it,' she said. 'You're not Superman, you have feelings, too.'

'All right.' His voice was defiant. 'I'm scared.'

'I should think you are,' she murmured. 'Most people are terrified.'

'So what do I do about it? I could take pills—but I refuse to.'

'There's a little technique I use,' she said, 'when I'm feeling down. I remember happy times in the past. It's somewhere I can go back to in my mind. I've got a cousin who lives out on a farm in Derbyshire, she has a little caravan where I used to stay with my mother. The farm's just under a wood on the top of the hill and you can see all of Buxton below. It's lovely just to sit outside there and watch. You must have something like that?'

'There's no place. I'll create somewhere, a sort of composite. But it'll include people.'

In fact, Tania's memory had included her much-loved mother, but that bit of the account she had suppressed. 'Go on,' she said.

'It's on the beach, a place I know in Italy. I'm sitting in the shade, looking at the sea, a Campari in my hand. I'm in a pair of swimming shorts and by my side there's a young lady in a bikini. And I'm blissfully happy.'

'Who's the young lady?' she asked shakily.

'I don't know. I haven't found her yet. But I'll know her when I find her. Aren't all men looking for the perfect beauty?'

'I told you what I think. Beauty is found in the spirit, not the body.'

*   *   *

The following Monday they were trying the long-cane technique on the open road. If Jonathan walked out of the entrance to the flats and turned right he would eventually come to a kiosk that sold a little bit of everything. He was known at the kiosk because they used to deliver his papers.

'What do I do if I hear people coming towards me?' he asked.

'Move slowly, and make sure you have your cane in front of you. That shows you're blind. The great majority of people are decent. They'll keep out of your way.'

To get to the kiosk he had to cross one road. It wasn't a busy road—in fact, a cul-de-sac—but occasionally cars parked in it. Tania knew he must be feeling apprehensive, but he was determined to try to cross.

'Find your way to the edge of the pavement. Stand there and listen. You've got good hearing, you'll know when there's a car coming. Now, I'm not going to help you. You tell me when it's safe to cross.'

In fact, he was very good. He could tell which cars were passing straight along the main road, which were slowing down in preparation perhaps to turn into the cul-de-sac. 'I could do it on my own,' he said.

'No. A couple more trips with me and then you'll be ready. When Derrick caught you out on your own that time he was right to tell me off. And you were wrong to try it so soon.'

'I felt frightened in the car,' he confessed, 'so I had to do something to prove to myself that I was on top of things.'

'Do something like getting run over,' she said comfortably.

When they got to the kiosk he bought a bar of chocolate and they shared it companionably on the way back.

'It's your birthday next week,' he said, 'and you're going to be twenty-eight. Getting on a bit. Time you were planning, thinking about your future.'

She knew he was joking with her. 'It is my birthday,' she said primly, 'but you're not supposed to comment on a lady's age.'

'Perhaps not. May I just say then that you don't seem a day over twenty-one.'

'You may. And how did you find out my birth date?'

He grinned sheepishly. 'I asked Joe to find out. He's good at anything like that. With infectious diseases you often have to be a detective. You find out how a person was infected, trace possible contacts—it's very important. Now, I want to get you a present.'

'But, Jonathan, I—'

'Don't object! It will give me no end of pleasure. Now, it's not long before the dance we're going to. Have you got a dress for it?'

'I'll be able to find one,' she said. 'There'll be something in my wardrobe.' In fact, she did have one though she'd never worn it to a formal ball.

'Well, I'd like to buy a dress for you. I gather there's a place in town called Gowns. I'd like you to go with Joe and buy one.'

This was something she hadn't expected. It was a lovely idea—she would like a new ballgown—but she thought it led her into a new kind of relationship with Jonathan. She wanted it, of course—how she wanted it—but whether she would regret it eventually, she just didn't know.

'I'm not sure about you buying me anything,' she said, 'much less a ballgown. Just a birthday card would do. But still…how do you know about this place, Gowns, and why should Joe take me?'

'A good junior registrar anticipates his boss's every need,' he said. 'I mentioned ballgowns to him and he volunteered to go with you and found the best shop. I did think of asking Eleanor to go with you—but then I thought that would be undiplomatic.'

'You're all sensitivity,' she said.

'It would please me to buy you a dress, though.'

'But I've got one!'

'Let me guess. It'll be long, of course—but also high-necked and long-sleeved.'

She looked at him in astonishment. 'How did you know?'

'I guessed. But you have a gorgeous figure to go with a gorgeous face, so I want you to wear a gorgeous dress to go with them. This is purely selfish on my part. I want to be the man who has brought the best-looking girl to the ball. So may I ask Joe to go shopping with you?'

'I'm sure he's really looking forward to it,' she said.

CHAPTER SIX

TANIA had to phone to cancel their next appointment. There was a mass of paperwork in the office to catch up on, and so it was a few days before she called on Jonathan again. She found him in very high spirits.

'I've just had a wonderfully embarrassed phone call,' he said. 'It's quite put me in a good temper. The hospital Chief Executive Officer has had to call—he's a good chap, I feel a bit sorry for him. He tries to do his best in very often very difficult circumstances. Like me.'

'You're a man, not a circumstance!'

'I'm a circumstance as well. Anyway, apparently the hospital is responsible for my injuries. What I've suffered already could cost them thousands. And if I…suffer permanent damage then they'll be liable for much much more. Costs could go into millions.'

'That must be nice for you,' she muttered.

'It isn't. For a start, I wouldn't take more than the minimum I need. I've got some feelings for the NHS and I don't like this victim culture. Anyway, I hope it won't be necessary. Now, what's the matter with you?'

'Nothing's the matter with me! Why should it be?' She knew her voice sounded defensive and that made her angrier than ever.

They were sitting in the kitchen, having a coffee that he had made, before they started on the afternoon's work.

'Tania! I've told you, I'm getting good at hearing

what's underneath voices. Something's upsetting you and I want to know what it is.'

She hesitated. 'Promise not to get angry?'

'You're always asking me that! And it's hard to do if I don't know what it is. What if it's something I ought to get angry at?'

'Then that's your problem. I just can't deal with one of your tempers at the moment.'

Jonathan sighed. 'All right, I promise. Now what's wrong?'

'Well, for a start, this isn't Derrick's fault—I don't think so anyway. You know I've been living in the nurses' home at the school for the past twelve months? I'm not entitled to, and there are only four rooms altogether. Well, they've appointed a new nurse, and she wants the room. And she wants it soon.'

'So you have to go flat-hunting?'

'I do. It shouldn't be much trouble, though. I travel light, I don't need a big place.'

He was thoughtful. 'I see. You're sticking to your job, though? Not being scared off by Derrick?'

'Not at all. Not yet anyway, though I might move on soon.'

'And then what about us? What about me and you, Tania? Wouldn't you miss me if you went? I'd certainly miss you.'

She didn't even want to think about that. 'I suppose I'd keep in touch with old friends.'

'Friends? Aren't we more than friends?' She knew he was playing with her and she didn't know how to handle it.

'To be any more than friends would be taking advantage of your condition,' she said. 'We'll carry on as we are until...until...'

'Just say "until",' he advised. 'Tania, I know you think my judgement might be affected because I'm blind. I don't think it is. I love your company, I love being with you. But for the moment…I've got something else to think about.'

He brooded for a moment. Eventually he said, 'You remember how I paid you to go to dinner with me? Because you wanted me to be independent of you?'

'Something like that,' she said.

'Well, I'm going to make you another offer. Free board and lodgings here. In return you give me a certain number of hours' assistance.'

She had to admit to herself that her first reaction was excitement. She'd be living with Jonathan! But then she realised—no, it just wasn't possible.

As she was about to tell him this, he broke in. 'I'd like you to consider the advantages both to you and me. I admit, the greatest advantages are to me. I often need things read to me, professional journals and so on. You'd be of inestimable help. I know I'm making some progress, but if you were here all the time I know I'd make a lot more. You get a breathing space. It's somewhere to live, you can look around, take your time.'

'Now tell me about the disadvantages,' she said.

Jonathan grinned sourly. 'More for me than for you. You'd live in my house, once again in effect my employee. As you know, there's no way I could…'

'Take unfair advantage of me?' she suggested with a giggle.

'Whatever. It would mean that our relationship had to remain formal. Isn't that what you want?'

'I think it would be better,' she said, though she was uncomfortably conscious of a sense of disappointment.

'It's settled, then. We can discuss terms and conditions later and this can be as formal as you like.'

'I think it better if we both stick to that.'

'As you wish.' He turned his head towards her, and although she knew he was blind, she had the uncanny feeling that he was staring at her. 'Now, tell me exactly why you want things to remain formal.'

She was a private person, she didn't like talking about her feelings. It made her feel vulnerable. But she did want Jonathan to know exactly how she felt, it was important to her.

'I think we're getting to…know each other,' she said. 'But in spite of being the toughest man I've ever met, I know you're under stress. You don't know whether you'll be blind for the rest of your life or not. So no decision you make now is entirely safe. Especially any decision about your…well, your emotional life.'

'Anyone ever tell you that you're as hard as a lump of rock, Miss Richardson?' he asked sardonically. 'Although, I must say, it's one of the things I love about you. And as for getting to know each other, I think we both—'

The phone rang. By now Jonathan could find his way to it at once. 'Knight here,' he said curtly. Then his voice softened. 'Good to hear from you, Charles… A week on Saturday morning? Fine. And what do you expect to find?' Tania was watching him and she saw him wince at the reply, but when he spoke again his voice was still perfectly calm. 'How long before I'll be out? Good again. I'll be there… No, I've got Tania with me. Bye.' He replaced the receiver, his expression unreadable.

'Tell me,' Tania said.

'You've met Charles, the neurosurgeon. My friend. He wants to do a set of tests a week after the ball. Then he can decide what can and cannot be done in a full-scale operation.'

'Will there be any kind of decision?' she asked gently.

'Possibly. He might be able to tell that I'll certainly remain blind. Or he'll tell me there's a chance that I might regain my sight.'

'So, bad news or the same situation,' she said. 'How do you feel about it?'

'I'm glad things are getting done,' he said. 'I don't like doubt. Actually, Tania,' he went on after a moment, 'I'm terrified. And you're the only person I'd admit that to.'

She walked over to him, put her arms round him and hugged him. A loving non-sexual, comforting hug. He hugged her back. 'You're so good for me,' he whispered.

She would have stayed there for ever, feeling his strength and his warmth, enjoying the feel of his breath on her cheek, the rise and fall of his chest. But eventually he gently pushed her away.

'I think I need exercise, Tania,' he said. 'Could we go for a walk? I'd really like a run, but I know Joe is busy today. You don't run yourself?'

'Not like you do.' She was thinking, considering possibilities, rejecting the most far-fetched. She could tell he needed to run. Physical exercise was one of the best ways of coping with stress.

'Go and get into your running gear, put your tracksuit on,' she said. 'I've got an idea. You don't mind being whistled at, do you?'

'Not if it's a whistle of appreciation.' Jonathan went to change.

She drove him to the beach and then they walked along the sand. Eventually they found themselves again on the great expanse of flat sand where he had run before. Once again the place was deserted—hardly a person to be seen and only the distant sea's murmur to listen to.

He stripped off his tracksuit and did his stretching exercises. Then Tania turned him to face the sea, about half a mile away. 'Just run,' she said. 'Slowly at first and, remember, pick your feet up. But there's nothing to trip over or fall into.' She blew a blast on the whistle she always kept in the car. 'Listen for this. One blast means stop. Two blasts means turn left and run. Three blasts means turn right and run. Now I'm going to send you out and see if I can guide you back to me.'

She knew what a strain it would be on him. He was alone, he had no idea what he was running towards. There was no Joe tied to him to act as a guide. The human reaction was to slow down, to reach out to see what was coming.

As she had suggested, he set off slowly at first. But then she could see his confidence growing. He accelerated a little, the tentative jogging turning into an easy long-legged stride.

When he neared the sea she blew a blast and he stopped. She blew two more blasts and he turned to the left, ran easily, parallel to the waves. Then she blew two blasts again and he turned and made his way back inland again. It worked! A final two blasts and he turned, more or less towards her. He had described an almost perfect square. Then she stopped him, and hurried over. 'You did so well! Did you enjoy it?'

'A bit frightening at first,' he panted, 'but exciting for all that. Do you want to send me round again?'

He did two more big squares. But then he got too confident, tried to run too fast and fell sprawling in the sand. She ran over to him. 'Jonathan! Are you all right?'

He pulled himself upright, brushing the sand from his face and body. 'I'm fine. My fault, trying to be too clever. I was going to stop now, but I think I need to do another circuit.'

She looked at his sweat-gleaming body. The singlet and shorts now did little to conceal the proportions of that wonderfully muscled body. 'Don't you think you've done enough?' she asked. 'You look…warm.'

'Just taken a fall. I need to run again to make sure I don't lose my confidence.'

Another, essentially masculine idea. 'All right, then. But just to the sea and back. This time when I whistle, turn right round.'

He did as she suggested, then stood by her, wiping his face with the towel she handed him. 'Thank you so much,' he said. 'That was wonderful and just what I needed. Now, answer me a question. Are you going to move into my spare room?'

'Yes,' she said.

'Then the sooner the better. Will you move in to-night?'

'Yes,' she said again. But she wondered if she was doing a wise thing.

Moving out didn't take very long. Tania had expected to go at any time and she didn't have too many possessions. Two cases, four large cardboard boxes and she was packed. She drove to Jonathan's flat at once.

He had given her a key to the front door and the flat and a card to open the electronic garage, where she was to occupy his spare parking place. She took the lift up to his flat. Odd. There was no one there. But this at least gave her the chance to move in all her stuff. She knew he'd be desperate to help her and she'd rather do this herself.

After half an hour she had moved in. She had a quick shower. They had arranged that the main bathroom would be largely hers as Jonathan had an *en suite* bathroom opening off his bedroom. She put on a new light dress and went to look for him. Probably he would be in the garden, practising his long cane work.

It had been a hot day and it was still a warm evening. She saw Jonathan at once, though he had his back to her. He was wearing a white shirt and light grey trousers and, of all things, he had a panama on his head. He was sitting on one of the benches, and with him there was a girl, who also had her back to Tania. She was wearing a pink dress with a pink hat. Tania thought she had never seen anyone hold themselves so gracefully. She also thought she was a tiny bit jealous as Jonathan seemed entranced by what the girl was saying.

Tania walked towards the couple, crunching along the gravel path. When she neared them Jonathan turned his head and called, 'Good evening, Tania.'

She stopped, startled. 'How did you know it was me?'

'Your step on the gravel is unmistakable. I know the length of your stride, the way you put your foot down. I even heard the little hesitation when you saw I was with someone.'

'You're catching on fantastically quickly. With most people it takes months before they're as good as that.'

'Perhaps you have a distinctive footstep.'

Now Tania came to the front of the bench. Jonathan had already risen and the girl with him now did the same. But she wasn't a girl—she was a woman. Perhaps in her late fifties, a woman who had looked after herself and now knew how to use the best cosmetics to the best effect. Tania thought she had never seen anyone look so gorgeous. It wasn't just the dress, the figure and the face—though all were wonderful. When she smiled, there was a vitality about this woman that communicated itself instantly.

'I'm Marianne Knight—Jonathan's mother,' the woman said. 'Tania, I'm so glad to meet you. I gather you've been looking after my son.'

And that was the last delight. Marianne had a definite Yorkshire accent.

She leaned forward and kissed Tania—not an ethereal kiss into the air but a hug and a deliberate, proper kiss. 'Now, tell me what it's like, looking after him. I find it hard myself. You know, I only heard about this…this accident a couple of days ago. When I was in America. He didn't tell me till then.'

'Tania was the one that pushed me into phoning you, Mum. I thought if you knew you'd only fuss.'

'Well, of course I'd fuss! And now I'm here I'm going to. That's what mothers are for.'

There was obviously a great deal of affection between the two. Tania remembered her own happy relationship with her own mother, and for a moment felt envious. They were so happy with each other.

'Have you moved in yet?' Jonathan asked. 'I would have been there to meet you, but Mum arrived and —'

'I've taken my stuff upstairs. But since your mother's here, perhaps I ought to—'

'Don't you dare say you'll stay away,' Marianne interrupted. 'He may not need you, but I certainly will. You will stay, won't you?'

'I'd love to,' said Tania.

Marianne sat down, moving her skirt along the bench. 'Sit here by me,' she said. 'Jonathan's been telling me about you. He says you're honest and good for him. Now, tell me—he will get his sight back, won't he?'

It had been hidden so far, but now Tania could hear the anguish in her voice. 'Jonathan's getting the best possible attention,' she said. 'The neurosurgeon is one of the best in the country. If it can be done, he'll do it. And I can honestly say that Jonathan has been the best man I've ever come across at dealing with sudden blindness. If necessary, he'll cope.'

'You're so supportive.' Marianne smiled. 'But now, please answer my question.'

'The chances of him regaining his sight are about fifty-fifty,' Tania said flatly. Just saying it horrified her.

She saw the tears in Marianne's eyes.

Jonathan took his mother's hand. 'Don't let it get you down,' he said. 'Life goes on. Now, look as if you're pleased to see me.'

'I am pleased to see you,' said his mother. 'I just want you to see me back.'

Tania said. 'It's lovely out here in the sun. It's a bit late, but shall I fetch a tray of afternoon tea?'

'I'd like that,' said Jonathan.

'So long as it's clearly understood that next time I fetch it,' said Marianne.

*   *   *

It was Saturday morning and staying with Jonathan had worked out surprisingly well so far. She got on very well with Marianne—the two shared a sense of humour. And Marianne was sensitive. She didn't ask questions or probe into Tania's relationship with Jonathan. Instead, she gossiped about famous people she had met, and Tania was fascinated.

But now it was dress-buying time. Joe had been let off the job. At present he was at the hospital with Eleanor and Jerry O'Connor, the new locum consultant who had just started. Jonathan knew Jerry well as the two had worked together in the past. Jerry had visited Jonathan and the two had spent a long morning together. Now Jonathan was reasonably happy to hand over his department—if only for a time.

Marianne was to take Tania shopping. It was a job she said she was looking forward to, and Tania believed her. Marianne had an incredible dress sense— and many of the clothes she wore were simple chain store purchases. But by putting different things together she always managed an effect that was striking and unusual.

They took Tania's car to the city centre and walked into Gowns. Tania had never been in a shop like this, but Marianne was instantly at home. 'Shopping should be a pleasure that is taken slowly,' she told Tania. 'It is to be savoured. Never buy anything expensive in a rush.'

An assistant established Tania's size and led them to the rack of ballgowns. 'We'll browse for a while,' Marianne told her, 'then we'll ask for you.'

She turned a sharp eye on Tania, moved her into the sunlight. 'We must get something to bring out that dark colouring of yours,' she muttered. 'You can wear something striking—barbaric even. You've got a face that can take it. It's full of strength.'

That rather pleased Tania. It was obvious that Marianne wasn't trying to flatter her but was just taking the detached view of a woman who knew an awful lot about clothes.

Marianne went on, 'You have a glorious figure, too. You must feature that bust and that waist. They tell us that the weather is going to stay hot, so I suggest something a little bit daring.' She sniffed. 'To be honest, I don't think much of that dress you're wearing now. That high neckline! You never reveal too much, do you?'

'No,' said Tania. 'I don't like outfits that show too much. They're just not me.'

'But you have such good skin! You should show it!'

'No, please, I just don't like things like that.'

'Very well. Perhaps it's better to hint and suggest than to state.'

They looked at every dress and then selected half a dozen that might possibly do. The assistant put them all on a rack and then asked if the ladies would like a cup of tea or perhaps coffee. 'Coffee, I think,' said Marianne. 'It stimulates the brain more. Then we'll make our choice. Do you want me to be lady's maid, Tania, and help you change?'

That was the last thing Tania wanted. 'No,' she said hurriedly. 'You sit out here and I'll come to you.' Then she went into the changing cubicle and shut the door very firmly. Marianne mustn't see her undressed. She mustn't see the scarring.

Tania loved trying on all the dresses. She modelled them one by one, coming out of the cubicle, walking up and down, twisting round so Marianne could see the full effect. Marianne felt the fabrics, assessed the cuts. She found faults that Tania had never even noticed. And there was no need to hurry. This was something to be enjoyed at leisure.

Eventually they narrowed the choice down to two. There was a shimmery silk petrol blue dress, with fitted bodice and waist, spreading out into a bell skirt. It was held up with bootlace straps and had a short fitted jacket. Then there was a black dress in a soft floating fabric. There was a white underlayer beneath it, which showed at the neck and the hem. It was high at the front but with a lower-cut back and was split to mid-thigh.

'You would wear either of those and you'd be a sensation,' said Marianne, 'but I think you'd be a bigger sensation in the black. Don't forget, all the men will be in black and white, you'll be competing with them. If you know what I mean, that's a dangerous dress. Very few women could get away with wearing that. But you could.'

Tania looked at herself in the mirror, pirouetted and stared over her shoulder at the back view. Yes, this dress was really something. In the past few years she'd never done anything exciting like wearing a dress like this. 'I think I'll have this,' she said.

'You'll need new underwear,' Marianne said. 'Always dress well from the inside out. It makes you feel good. And we'll buy you some new shoes. Next department down, I think.'

Finally they finished shopping and their purchases were waiting for them in a set of shiny dark purple carriers. Tania caught a glimpse of the cheque Marianne signed and was horrified. 'I saw that,' she squeaked. 'I haven't spent that much on clothes in the past three years.'

'It's Jonathan's money and he can afford it,' Marianne said laconically. 'He rarely spends anything on himself. Now, all this spending is tiring. We'll have tea in the restaurant upstairs.'

'I'm going to cross-examine you now,' she said when they were sitting together in the shop's gold and white tearoom. 'It's a mother's privilege. My son—you know what he's going through, don't you?'

'I think so,' replied Tania. 'In fact, I know so. He tries to keep up this front of being hard, but he's human, like the rest of us. It's just that he makes it difficult for anyone to get through to him. Perhaps it's his way of coping.'

'Perhaps it is.' Marianne was obviously not sure about something. 'I've just been offered a big contract in New York, work that'll take me all my time for the next four months. I want to turn it down, to stay with Jonathan—to look after him, if you like. But I'm not sure if that would be good for him. What do you think, Tania?'

She hadn't expected this. 'You shouldn't ask me,' she said firmly. 'I'm not a doctor. I don't know what's best.'

'I don't want a doctor's opinion. I want an answer from someone who's close to him. The question is, will it be better for Jonathan if I stay here and mother him, or if I go and leave him to fight his own battles?'

'You could ask him!'

'And you know very well what he'd say. This is a decision I need to take without consulting my son.'

It was some time before Tania could force herself to speak. She sensed that Marianne knew how the question was troubling her, how hard she found it to answer. Finally, she managed to get the words out. 'You shouldn't ask me questions like that. I might be wrong, and that would be dreadful. And I like you. But I think that at the moment Jonathan needs…space. Whatever happens, he needs to manage it on his own.'

Marianne sighed. 'I thought you'd say that but I was hoping you wouldn't. The thing is, I agree with you. I'm to love him but keep my distance for a while.'

She bent her head to sip her tea. Tania thought she caught a glimpse of a tear.

But when Marianne asked her next question, she was as tough as ever. 'Tell me, how often do the people you help fall in love with you?'

'Occasionally,' Tania said. 'Actually, it tends to be the older ones.' She giggled. 'I have had a proposal—not of marriage unfortunately—from an eighty-year-old. But mostly it's not love so much as reliance.'

'And are you bound by the—what is it—Hippocratic oath? You swear not to take sexual advantage of your patients?'

'We don't take the Hippocratic oath,' Tania explained. 'We're not doctors or nurses but trainers. We don't call them patients but clients. But I'd like to think that we feel the same way about those we're trying to help. I can think of nothing worse than taking advantage of someone who is blind.'

'So do you worry about you and Jonathan? Do you think you're being fair to him?'

'Yes, I worry,' Tania admitted. 'And sometimes I think that Jonathan's not being fair to me. But I do think that I'm helping him.'

'You certainly are. And don't worry about breaking

his heart. It won't be bad for him, to feel what his girlfriends in the past have suffered.'

'I don't want to hurt him. But there are two things about us. First, in general, I don't want to get married. Second, well, he's blind. His well-ordered life is upside down. He thinks he's tough, and he probably is, but he's still vulnerable. There's a danger that he'll fall for anyone who will show him sympathy and kindness. He may well get his sight back. And after that I doubt whether I'll see much more of him.'

'I'm sure you will,' replied Marianne. 'You're a very beautiful young woman.'

CHAPTER SEVEN

'I DON'T think ballroom dancing is part of our necessary curriculum,' Tania said on the following Monday, 'although I know they have dances on our club afternoons.'

'Well, it should be part of the curriculum. It teaches you to be confident and rhythmic. Didn't I once see a film starring Robert de Niro when he was a blind dancer?'

'I think there is one,' she said. 'I've never seen it. Do you like dancing?'

'The little I've done I've enjoyed very much. Now, is there a socket we can use or do we have to rely on the batteries?'

They were in the church hall she used for long-stick training. Jonathan was holding a cardboard box that held a portable player and a set of CDs, which he had refused to let her carry.

'I think there's a socket over here,' she said. She led him to the corner of the stage and plugged in the player. 'Now, what shall we start with?'

'Well, Joe's made a few enquiries and I remember what happened last year. There'll be a band and a lot of the music will be formal—you know, the old-fashioned waltz and quickstep and so on. Then in the intervals there will be a disco for the younger and more adventurous dancers. I suspect this time I'd better give the disco dancing a miss.'

'You're probably right. The sight of you gyrating on your own…'

'Not a pretty sight and probably dangerous to passers-by,' he said. 'I entirely agree. We'll stick to the older stuff. You know, the bit where I get to hold you.'

'That,' she told him, 'is not the aim of the exercise.' She looked through the box of CDs. 'Shall we start with something slow and easy—a waltz?'

'A waltz would be fine. Nice, romantic music. Vienna and Strauss and so on.'

'Viennese waltzing? We're not going to move that quickly quite just yet.' She picked out a CD and slid it into the player.

The music echoed across the hall, and Jonathan stood there and opened his arms. After a moment's hesitation Tania moved into them. She took his left hand in her right, his right hand slid round her waist. The classic dancing position.

'The gentleman is supposed to lead,' he said, 'guiding the lady by subtle pressure and the movement of his body. How are we going to manage if you're moving backwards all the time?'

'I'll look over my shoulder,' she told him. 'Don't worry, we won't mow anyone down.'

'I think I'd better get closer to you. That way I'll feel safer.' Gently, he pulled her body to his.

'Why do I think that your mind isn't entirely on dancing?'

'I've no idea. All I want to do is perfect another physical skill. Now, one two three, one two three…' And they were away.

He was accustomed to leading, and it was hard for him to learn to follow her. And she was accustomed to being led. The first couple of minutes were farcical, as each tried to adopt the other's role. But slowly they learned to move together. And it had to be together. It was easiest if their bodies were close, touching.

He was a quick study. And she learned her new part quickly, being able to direct him, slow him, weave their way through imaginary other couples. When they thought they had mastered the waltz they moved on to the foxtrot and the quickstep. It got easier.

Tania found herself enjoying the music, the ease of movement, in a way she hadn't enjoyed herself in years. This was a new physical skill for Jonathan, and he brought to it the concentration and the determination she had seen in all his other learning. Soon they were both enjoying themselves.

They danced for two hours. But then it was time to get back to the flat. Marianne would have a meal waiting for them. 'I want to be traditional,' he said. 'Put on a last waltz, and I'll ask you if I can walk you home. Or I'll even get us a taxi.'

'You certainly know how to show a girl a good time. But the sexes are equal now. I'll drive you home.'

The last waltz spun to a close. They stood together in the middle of the floor, sunlight flooding through the windows shining on the stacked chairs, the faint dusty smell around them. It wasn't the romantic setting suggested by the music, but for a moment Tania wouldn't have been anywhere else.

He didn't release her. Instead, he slid his left arm round her waist so he was holding her loosely, face to face. And when he stooped to kiss her she pulled him closer to her. It started as just a friendly kiss, an acknowledgement of time spent together, holding each other. But then it deepened into something more.

Jonathan took his arms from round her waist and

touched her face. She held him still. His fingertips ran down her cheeks, outlined her lips, glided gently over her neck. A caress so gentle, so sweet as to be almost unendurable.

'I think I can see by touching,' he said hoarsely, 'and I know that you're beautiful.'

His hands followed her arms, stroking the insides of her elbows. Then his thumbs rubbed her wrists. All so sweet. He placed his hands on her waist and she felt his hesitation.

'Go on,' she said. 'I don't mind, really I don't. In fact, I would like it.' She didn't recognise the voice as hers.

His hands strayed down the front of the thin T-shirt she was wearing, held her breasts. She knew that her nipples awoke, reacted to his touch. It excited her as much as it excited him.

'You're so beautiful,' he breathed again. 'Do you realise, the reason I most want my sight back is so that I can see you—all of you?'

'That's a lovely thing to hear,' she said, her voice almost breaking under the strain.

Tania realised she had been swimming round the edges of a whirlpool, thinking she was safe. Now she knew she wasn't. She had been dragged into the vortex.

'We're going to have a little party before the ball,' Jonathan said late on that day. 'Just cocktails, and I've arranged for a tray of small nice things to be brought in. There'll be eight of us and we'll have a table together. I've left all this arranging to Joe here.'

'As if I don't have enough to do,' said Joe, who had dropped in for a visit. 'Look at me. Rushed off my feet.' In fact, he was lying full length on the couch in

Jonathan's living room, a glass of orange juice balanced on his chest.

'If he does well,' Jonathan went on remorselessly, 'then in time he gets to be important like me. If he doesn't do well, it's corn plasters for the rest of his life.'

'A good corn-plasterer brings joy to many people,' Joe pointed out. 'However—'

'Who are the rest of the eight?' Tania broke in. She had learned that the only way of getting an answer when Joe and Jonathan were in this mood was to interrupt.

'There's you and me,' Jonathan said. 'Joe and…Joe?'

'I have found an attractive nurse companion,' Joe said, 'called Jenny Lee. She's the probationer on our ward. Only when I got to know her did I realise we have so much in common. She trained as a chef for a while. She likes cooking and I like eating.'

'Obviously a partnership made in heaven,' Tania said. 'Who else?'

'Senior Registrar Eleanor Page and the new locum consultant, Jerry O'Connor,' said Joe. 'Moved in fast there did our Eleanor. A good career move.'

'Just professional courtesy,' Jonathan said. 'Don't be bitter, Joe. Did she turn you down?'

Joe was horrified. 'Me? Turned down by Eleanor!'

'Now I know how men talk behind women's backs,' Tania said disapprovingly. 'You're all terrible gossips. Who's the fourth couple?'

'My mother and my surgeon,' Jonathan said. 'Marianne phoned Charles Forsythe and asked to talk to him. And now they so much enjoy talking about me that they're going to do it in public.'

Tania could tell by his amiable tone that Jonathan thought this coupling was an excellent idea. 'I like Charles,' she said. 'He's good company.'

'Incidentally,' Jonathan went on, 'my Mum's having her personal hairdresser come here to see to her on the afternoon of the ball. She wants to know if you'd like your hair done, too.'

'Well, I was going to go to a nurse I know,' Tania said, 'but it would be a lot easier to have it done here.' She had never had a hairdresser come to the house.

'I've to tell you that she can do your make-up as well,' Jonathan said. 'Perhaps she'll do mine, too.'

The day of the dance was hot. In the morning Jonathan sat with Tania in the garden and she read to him from the journals he needed for his work. It was surprisingly enjoyable. He didn't just listen, he commented. And what he said was always interesting.

She was just opening a new magazine when a full-page advertisement caught her eye. 'Jonathan!' she squeaked. 'It's got your name here!' She looked through the rest of the page. 'There's a symposium in Florida—the American Association of Communicable Diseases—and you're supposed to be talking about the spread of tuberculosis in Britain and how visitors from abroad have affected this spread.'

'A few years ago we thought we had tuberculosis beaten,' he told her calmly. 'Now there are signs of it coming back. Olive was only one of many cases I've come across.'

'But what are you going to do?' She looked at the page again. 'The meeting starts in a fortnight.'

'Well, I've already written the talk, that's no problem. But I want to present it myself.' He sat there, contentedly enjoying the morning sunshine, and said, 'I've been meaning to ask you but I wanted to wait for the right time. Would you like to come to Florida with me, Tania?'

'What?'

'Quite a few of the delegates take secretaries or research assistants or even wives and partners with them,' he said. 'You'd be acting as a kind of secretary for me. Taking notes here and there, lists of addresses and so on. And you'd be my eyes, telling me what was happening.'

'You want me to go as a secretary? We'll need to set firm boundaries and agree on my role now. We need to get that straight.'

'Sadly, secretary is all,' he said. 'I was going to take Joe, but he can't be spared from the department.'

'I don't know what to say,' she muttered. 'Tell me more about what I'd have to do.'

'Well, you'd have to read my speech and—'

'Read your speech! Stand up in front of all those people and read your speech? Couldn't someone else do that?'

'I suppose they could. But if you read it, I feel it would be personal to me. I'd be sitting by you on the stage. Afterwards there are always questions and I'd answer those. It would only take about half an hour, Tania. We could rehearse it together. Will you come?'

'Well, I'd love to go to Florida,' she said, 'I've never been to America.'

'You'd be a wonderful help to me,' he said. 'No one knows better than you what I can do, what I can't. Of course, I'd pay you, so it would be entirely proper.'

'Does your paying me stop you from trying to sleep with me?' she asked boldly.

'You know very well it does. That's why you want
to be paid, and it's also why I want to pay you.'

Jonathan stopped a moment, and Tania realised
they'd strayed into an area far from whether she would
go to Florida or not. It was something she had to keep
reminding herself of. This man was too good at hiding
his feelings. Often she had no idea what his thoughts
were, what he was going through.

He said, 'I want everything from you except pity.
And you could sleep with me out of pity.'

'It's not very likely,' she said tartly. 'I'm not sure I
want to sleep with anyone yet. But other than that,
don't you think that I'm entitled to give what I want
to who I want? And for whatever reason? In a few
weeks' time you'll be either blind for life or able to
see. My feelings towards you won't be changed by
either, I assure you.'

'You told me just how much being newly blind
could affect people's judgement,' he said. 'I believed
you. I may be wrong about you, but I still think you're
capable of being motivated by pity. And that I won't
have. Now, let's change the subject. It's really hot, but
above all I'd like to go for a run.'

'I'll get my whistle,' she said.

There would be no decision about Florida yet.

There were more people on the sands today, but it was
still too early for it to be really crowded. One or two
looked curiously when they saw her standing there,
blowing her whistle at the running man. But it was easy
to direct Jonathan to avoid them. Finally, when he was
streaming with sweat, he ran into the sea. For a couple
of minutes he bathed there, rolling over and over in the
surf. Tania was worried and ran closer to the sea. But

she saw that he was in no danger. The waves showed him where the water's edge was.

Back at the flat Jonathan showered, and then Joe called to take him to the hospital. It had been decided that the flat should be left to the two women in the afternoon. 'We'd only be in the way,' Jonathan had said.

Tania had a lovely, self-indulgent afternoon. Eunice, Marianne's old friend and hairdresser, came round. After seeing to Marianne, she went to look at Tania's new dress. Then she took her long hair and dressed it in ringlets that would cascade down her back. It was a style Tania had seen and admired but had never dared to try herself. And when Eunice had finished, she suggested a new shade of lipstick for Tania, showed her how to accentuate her eyes to make them look more feline, almost oriental. 'Marianne said you had a strong face,' she said, 'and you have. You can get away with effects that would just not suit a weaker woman.'

When Eunice left Marianne said she would go to her room to sleep for a while as it was going to be a long night. Tania thought this a good idea; however, she couldn't sleep herself. She was excited, unsettled. But there was no way she could think about her problems. They seemed insoluble.

She heard voices outside and knew Joe and Jonathan had returned. She stayed in her room, intending not to come out until she had heard Marianne make her entrance. Other people arrived and then it was time. She slid into her dress, adjusted it, put on her make-up. And walked out.

Jonathan was there, looking impeccable in a classic dinner jacket. The white and black outfit suited him very well. All the others were there. She had met them all except Jenny, Joe's escort. She was among friends—or at least acquaintances.

'Tania, that dress is magnificent. You look absolutely gorgeous.'

Of all people, it was Eleanor who spoke first, and Tania saw the compliment was genuine. 'Thank you,' she said. Well, the dress was gorgeous.

Someone handed her a drink and there were little hors d'oeuvres for them all to nibble at. After a while she found herself next to Jonathan. 'I can't see, but no fewer than three other people have assured me that you look absolutely stunning,' he whispered. 'I know you're going to be the belle of the ball, and I know every man in the ballroom will envy me.'

'It's only the dress that you bought for me,' she whispered back.

'No. The dress may be good, but it's only the setting for a jewel. Joe has promised me that we can have a photograph taken.'

They sat, chatted, sipped their drinks for a while. Then it was time to go and Joe said that their car was waiting downstairs. They ignored the lift, trooping down the stairs together and out to the drive.

'Oh, my Lord,' said Tania.

'What's wrong?' asked Jonathan impatiently. But she was looking at the others, realising they were as dumbstruck as she was.

'It's the car Joe has picked,' she said. 'I believe it's called a stretch limo.'

'If I ever get married,' Jenny said, 'I don't want to arrive or depart in one of those.'

It was a shiny, white, polished vehicle, incredibly long and with darkened windows. The driver stepped out and opened a selection of doors. 'I find a touch of bad taste every now and again to be refreshing,' said Joe. 'Let's get inside and pretend to be gangsters.'

So they did. It was comfortable inside, air-conditioned and with ample room for all their legs. 'Champagne?' asked Joe, opening a small fridge and taking out a gold-topped bottle.

The ball was being held at the Yelland Country Club, a large house some distance out of town. They were met at the door and escorted to their table, one of many round the polished floor. She was pleased to notice that this room was also air-conditioned, otherwise the heat would have been intolerable.

It was a night Tania knew she would remember. She sat next to Jonathan, whispering a commentary to him, telling him who was approaching, how everyone was dressed, how their group was managing.

Then they danced. The first time around the floor wasn't successful—Jonathan reverted to wanting to lead. But things improved when he relaxed and she led, and they whirled round the floor like a couple of experts.

Tania was asked to dance by the other men on their table. It was rather funny as she had to explain that the reason things weren't going too well was because she was trying to lead.

'You took Jonathan to practise?' Charles said. 'That shows forethought, a great deal of imagination. If ever you think of a career in hospital—any kind of career—let me know.' She took that as a compliment.

There was no set meal—instead, waiters placed a succession of light dishes on the table in front of them and people were invited to help themselves to what they wanted. Tania told Jonathan what was available;

he was pleased that he didn't have to make his way through a heavy formal meal.

She hadn't realised just how popular Jonathan was. Many people came to the table to wish him well, shake his hand and buy him a drink. Soon the table was nearly covered with glasses. 'I'll get rid of a few of these,' Joe said. 'Wouldn't want people getting the wrong impression, would we?'

It was a good table to be at. There was a variety of experience there, a variety of stories to be told. Jerry had just come back from working in Africa. He had them alternatively amused and horrified by what he had seen. Marianne appeared to have met everyone of note in the fashion world and didn't hesitate to reveal the latest scandals. Jenny had been a chef before she'd trained to be a nurse. She had them all determined never to eat in a restaurant again! Yes, a good table to be at.

'Why are you so quiet?' Tania asked Jonathan when they were dancing once more. 'You're as clever as all these people, I've heard you be just as funny.'

His answer rather shocked her, reminded her that she still had much to learn. 'I can talk perfectly well to one person or two, but many more than that is difficult. You can't tell who's going to speak next. You need to see people's faces to know how well they're going along with you.'

'Oh,' she said. 'I'm afraid I didn't quite realise that.'

Jonathan squeezed her hand. 'It doesn't matter. Because of you, Tania, I'm having the time of my life. I'm actually enjoying this, not enduring it. And now, as we dance, I can feel what those around me are thinking. The women are all jealous of you and the men are all envious of me.'

'Flatterer,' she said. But she had to admit to herself that she had noticed more than a few masculine glances that suggested that her outfit, well, made the most of her.

There was one serious note. Choosing a moment when their table was nearly empty, Charles said he wanted a quiet word with Jonathan. 'Tania, please, stay and listen if you like,' Charles said to her. 'In a sense it concerns you. Jonathan, we're quite close. I'm wondering if I ought to perform this operation. Are you sure you wouldn't rather have a surgeon who knows you less well? I can recommend half a dozen as competent as myself, if not more so.'

'I want you, Charles,' Jonathan said instantly. 'I've watched you work. Once you start you'll forget who I am completely. I'll just be a brain to you then.'

'All right. I'll do it if you wish. But if you change your mind, that's fine by me.'

'Excuse me,' Tania said, 'I'm interested in this. Could I ask a question? Charles, when you operate do you really forget about the person you're working on?'

Charles mused for a minute. 'To a certain extent, yes,' he said. 'You've done all your homework, you know the patient, you've seen the X-rays, the scans, the results of any previous treatment. You've a good idea of the chances of success of an operation, also of its dangers. You know the consequences of not performing an operation—usually you've discussed this with the patient. You're bound to get some sort of…fellow feeling for the person. If you can't feel sympathy you're not good as a doctor. But once you've made the first cut with the scalpel all thought of consequences must disappear. You focus solely on the work.'

'I see,' said Tania. 'It sounds very lonely work.'

'I've never thought of it that way,' said Charles after a moment. 'But I suppose it is.'

The ball didn't go on too late. For a start, many of those there would be needed in hospital the next day. In all too short a time the evening was coming to an end. But not for everyone. Tania was fascinated to hear where the various couples were disappearing to. Eleanor was taking Jerry to a nightclub in town. Marianne was going for a late supper and then staying the night with Charles, who had a large house some distance away. Jenny was taking Joe home to feed him.

'It's just like when we were teenagers at the end of a dance,' she muttered to Jonathan. 'Everybody cops off.'

'What a vulgar expression! And we're just a boring old couple who need to go to bed with our cocoa,' said Jonathan. 'Come on, Tania, it'll soon be hot-water-bottle time.'

'Not tonight it won't,' Tania said.

In fact, they had received several invitations, to parties, suppers and so on. Jonathan had asked her each time but they'd decided that the evening at the ball was enough. She knew it would have been tiring for him. So they went home alone. The ever-efficient Joe had arranged a car for them.

It had been a lovely hot day and evening, but now the weather showed signs of breaking. When they got outside the air felt thick and sticky and there was no wind. Neither were there any stars, and the sky was very black.

'I think we'll have a storm soon,' said Jonathan.

'It can't be soon enough,' she said.

Once back in the flat they both changed into something light and loose. Although they had enjoyed their evening, were tired even, they both felt a little dissatisfied. 'It's the still air,' Jonathan said. 'We'll feel differently when it starts to rain.' And after a while he said, 'Would you like to go for a walk in the garden?'

'I'd love it,' she said.

Outside the air was as sticky as ever. They walked along the gravel paths in the garden—by now Jonathan knew the garden so well he could find his way anywhere. They were in complete darkness, only two small lights shining from the flats. It was interesting. Now Jonathan was guiding her, not the other way round.

They came to a secluded bench in the furthest reach of the garden. There was a high wall behind them, bushes to the side and a tiny lawn in front of them. They sat and he put his arm round her. It might be hot, but she liked it. The first heavy drop of rain landed on her forehead.

'It won't be long now,' he said, and she shuddered. It wouldn't be long now.

It seemed a long time before the next drop. But then it landed with a noisy smack on the bench next to her. They both felt the faintest of breezes, but this time a breeze bringing freshness. Drop, drop, drop. The rain was rattling on the leaves of the bush next to her, still single heavy drops, smacking into her bare flesh. 'Do you want to go in?' he asked. 'We're going to get wet.'

'I want to get wet. Will you stay out here with me, Jonathan?'

'Oh, yes,' he said.

Then the storm passed. She could hear the murmur of thunder, see the flicker of lightning over the Welsh hills. And Tania and Jonathan sat on in the rain.

'This is wonderful,' he said, 'but I want to feel the

rain on all my skin.' Raising his arms, he pulled off his shirt. All she could see was a dark figure. 'That's wonderful,' he said. 'Why don't you do the same?'

She sat there a moment longer, in silence. Then he reached forward. His hands touched her waist, then felt for her thin shirt, easing it upwards and over her head. He dropped it on the bench beside him. Then, still cautiously, he leaned forward to unfasten her bra.

She knew she could stop him. One word, one hint and he would stop. But she didn't want to stop him. Her heart was hammering, with excitement and apprehension, but she wasn't going to stop him. It was wonderful to be naked next to him. The rain prickled at her skin, ran between her breasts, and she loved it.

His arm was still round her and he pulled her gently closer. She knew she still had a choice. She could pick up her clothes and say they should go in—or she could stay. And then what would happen? For too much of her life she had been running, hiding. Now she wanted a change. For once she would do something foolish. For once she would act without thinking of the consequences.

Perhaps Jonathan had guessed what she had been thinking, had given her time. That was kind of him. But now he put her arms round his neck and pulled her to him. His wet lips came down onto hers. His body pressed against her, she felt her breasts tight against him, she felt the excitement start there, drive throughout her body. They were wet, the cool rain still hissing down on them. But both were warmed by a fire that came from inside.

This was no ordinary kiss, tender or gentle. Jonathan's mouth was demanding, passionate. His tongue probed deep within her. She clutched the back of his head, holding his wet hair, and pulled him even closer. She could tell how much he wanted her!

They had been sitting side by side on the bench. He tugged at her so they slid downwards to lie side by side on the grass. Under her it was wet and cool and she didn't mind a bit. The rain was a gentle caress on her body that couldn't dampen the heat of their passion.

For a while they lay there side by side, their bodies pressed together as if nothing could ever part them. But then he eased her onto her back, and his head roamed over her body, taking each breast into his mouth, causing her back to arch in ecstasy. This was so good. But it wasn't enough!

Now his hands were at the elasticated waistband of her trousers. For a moment he hesitated, but she lifted her hips, and with one swift movement she was naked.

For a moment there was a touch of fear. What was she doing? But then she decided she had started on a course that must be finished. This was what she wanted.

He leaned back, there was the rustling of clothing and she sensed rather than saw that he was naked, too. Then his body was on hers again. 'Tania,' he muttered. 'Darling Tania, do you want to…? I don't know if…'

She reached for him. 'I'm yours, Jonathan,' she murmured. 'Put your arms round my neck. Whatever you do, don't move them. I need you to hold me just like that.'

Then he was on top of her. She could feel his entire body against hers, knew the strength of his desire for her, wanted so much to give herself to him. It seemed so proper in this storm that their desires should be as elemental as the forces of Nature that thrashed around them. She wriggled under him, every nerve ending in her body sensitised. She thought she could feel each blade of grass, each drop of rain that touched her body. And she knew every inch of his body, too, as it touched hers.

Then he knelt up, left her. Alarmed, she reached out towards him. 'Jonathan, what is it? Where are you?'

His voice was harsh. 'We should stop here. Apart from anything else, I haven't got anything.' He could even joke. 'It's hard to find your way around the men's room when you're blind.'

'It doesn't matter.' She knew what Jonathan meant at once and it made her love him the more because even at that moment he could think of her and the possible consequences. 'It doesn't matter, Jonathan. I'm always regular—very regular—and right now my chances of getting pregnant are nil. Jonathan, you can come back to me if you want!'

He came to her again, and for a while she was content just to be held by him again, just to have so much of his body pressed close to hers. But they both wanted—they both needed—more. She spread her legs wide apart, a universal gesture of offering. For a moment he was poised over her—and then slowly he lowered himself onto her, into her. There was a hesitation. 'But, Tania, you're a…'

He mustn't stop now. She gripped him, pulled him hard to her, forced her hips up to him. Then she sighed. The pain was tiny, and now they were to…

It didn't take long. She felt his urgency matching her own, their bodies seeming to take control, to do what they would. And then, explosive and sudden, a joint cry of ecstasy.

Tania wanted so much to say that she loved him.

But still she dared not—not yet. So they lay there, the rain washing at them.

Of course, they had to get back to the flat. And they couldn't do that stark naked. If they were seen, what might the neighbours think? There were wet clothes scattered by them, all had to be pulled on with difficulty.

'Seems a bit silly to dress when we're going to undress again so quickly,' he grumbled amiably, 'but I suppose the conventions must be obeyed.'

'We can say we got caught out in the storm,' she told him. 'That's perfectly true.'

'But it's not the whole story, is it?'

She kissed him. 'Come on. I'll feel better when we're inside.'

In fact, they met no one in the entrance or in the lift. Within minutes they were back in the flat, and now she had to start thinking. She knew very well what he would want—and, in fact, it was the same as she would want—but it just wasn't possible.

'Go and have a shower,' she told him. 'Put on a dressing-gown and come out here and I'll do the same. We need to talk.'

'That sounds ominous,' he said gently. 'First thing, Tania, actions speak louder than words. What we've just done, what we've just had—we can't explain that away.'

'I know. I wouldn't want to and I wouldn't try to. It meant so much to me, Jonathan. But still we must talk.'

'Well, come and have a shower with me. Or we could get in the bath together. Tania, I just want to touch and to hold you.'

'No,' she said firmly. 'Shower and get dry first, then we talk. Talk nicely. Jonathan…this was my first time, with any man. And I still don't know quite what it means. To you or me.'

'All right,' he said, 'we'll talk. But afterwards—we have the flat to ourselves. Will you come to my bed for tonight?'

How she ached to say yes! But she dared not. 'Shower,' she said. 'Or you'll catch your death of cold.' Then she went to the bathroom herself.

They sat side by side on the couch, cups of cocoa on the coffee-table in front of them. It was one of the silly things that bound them together—they both loved cocoa last thing at night to drink.

Jonathan had wrapped a short dressing gown round himself and he looked keen, alert, his damp hair tousled. There was a glint in his eyes—and Tania could have wept. He had beautiful eyes. And his brain wouldn't use them.

She had dug out her winter-weight dressing-gown in blue towelling. It fitted tight to her neck, descended to her feet. She felt safe, protected in it. But she didn't want to feel safe or protected.

'I know you'll think this is silly,' she said, 'but if you've got any regard for me you'll do as I say. First of all, I agree with you—what we did was wonderful.. I don't regret a minute, it'll be something that I'll carry with me to the end of my days. But we're not going to go any further now. Soon we'll know if you get your sight back or not. It won't make any difference to me. It might make a difference to you. So can we put things on hold till then? Please, Jonathan?'

He frowned, and she wondered what he was thinking. Then he said, 'If that's what you want then, of course, that's what we'll do. Though it's going to be hard for me!'

'It'll be hard for me, too,' she said. 'I've got feelings as well, Jonathan.'

'Don't I know it!' He grinned. 'Sorry, Tania, mustn't get carried away. So we won't do it again, and I guess you're going to tell me that it mustn't be mentioned again.'

'That's right,' she said.

'Then let me say just two things. Whatever happens, whether I get my sight back or not, I'll feel the same way about you, Tania. I love you. And if I do get my sight back, there's one thing I'm looking forward to. The sight of you, waiting for me, naked on my bed. It'll be the most wondrous thing I've ever seen.'

It took all her strength. She wanted so much to believe him. But once he had seen her disfigured body... 'I'm looking forward to lying there waiting for you,' she lied.

CHAPTER EIGHT

TANIA seemed to weep through most of the night. She lay in bed, her fingers running down her body, following the change from the smoothness of the skin on her waist, her breasts, her thighs, to the shiny roughness of the scar tissue on her abdomen. It was horrible! If she lay naked on Jonathan's bed, as she'd promised, he wouldn't see the perfect body he had imagined. What he would see was ugly, monstrous! Never would she give him the chance. Already, one man she'd thought she'd loved had been repulsed. It wouldn't happen again.

On Sunday morning she rose early, spent time in the bathroom soaking her eyes with cold water. He wouldn't see that she had been crying. When she returned, Marianne might.

She made coffee and he ambled out of his bedroom in his dressing-gown. 'Other people's coffee always smells better than my own,' he said. 'May I have a cup and will you give me a kiss?'

'Your chair's in the window,' she said, and watched him navigate to it expertly. Then she brought over coffee for both of them, and kissed him quickly on the cheek. 'That'll do for now,' she said, evading his grab. 'Sit there quietly, have your drink and we'll talk.'

'Actions speak louder than words. We're alone here. Come and kiss me again.' Then she saw doubt cover his face. 'You said you didn't want to talk about last night,' he said. 'Are you having second thoughts?'

'Far from it. Last night was…well, it was incredible. But I think we've been getting just a bit too emotional. I want us to enjoy each other's company. Just take pleasure in being with each other. Jonathan, it won't be for long!'

'Then we'll do as you wish.' He frowned again. 'Just one thing, though. Last night, you said everything was all right. But if there are any, well, unforeseen consequences, I—'

'If I'm pregnant, Jonathan,' she told him, 'you'll be the first to know.'

He sighed. 'You really do make better coffee than me,' he said.

After that they had an easy day. They went into the garden again and she read to him. For a while they listened to the radio together. Marianne came back by taxi in the early afternoon and said she'd had a wonderful time.

'You've had time to think,' Jonathan said casually after Marianne had left. 'Are you going to come to America with me?'

Tania had thought about it and had decided. It might cause her ultimate pain but the present pleasure was too much to give up. 'Yes, I'll come to America with you,' she said. 'I'm really looking forward to it.'

'Then we can rehearse my speech.' Jonathan stood, made his way to his work desk, pulled out a folder. She had noticed that he was the tidiest of men. It made being blind a little easier. Everything he owned had its place, and was in its place.

He handed her the folder. 'Read it through to yourself first. Then ask me any questions you want about it—you'll read it so much better if you understand everything. Then you can read it out loud.'

She did as he said. There were some concepts she didn't quite understand, some words she didn't know how to pronounce. But he explained and it all began to make sense.

After half an hour she said she'd like to try to read it. He made her stand at the other side of the room and pretend she was talking to an audience. At first she stumbled a bit, but soon she got used to the reading.

'You were good,' he said when she had finished, 'but you had the usual fault of people who read others' work—you spoke too quickly. Try the first page again.'

Since they'd first met, she had been his trainer, the expert showing him what to do. It seemed odd to have the roles reversed. But she liked it.

Tania had work the next day so she excused herself and went to bed early. She was tired and there were things she had to think about.

The time she had known Jonathan seemed to have passed with tremendous speed. Another week had flown by and now, next Monday, she was to go to Florida with Jonathan for a five-day stay. A week after they returned he was to have his operation. She had already booked herself leave, starting next Monday. She wanted to be with Jonathan when he came to after the operation, when he first knew whether he had re-gained his sight or not. If he hadn't, she wanted to be with him for the first few days. If he had regained his sight—and how she hoped that he would—then she didn't know what she would do. But she was on a part-timer's contract. She could leave at any time.

Carrying on as if things were normal was the hardest thing she had ever done. She visited a newly happy Olive. She was allocated Muriel Chalmers, a lady who had just been registered as completely blind. Muriel had been losing her sight for years so it shouldn't have come as a shock to her. But it did. Tania spent far more than the proper time, trying to get Muriel to do the basic minimum for herself.

Life in the flat was much more fun. Jonathan seemed to have accepted that they would have a quiet life. And she knew that even though there was the trip to Florida first, he must be worrying about his operation. The alternatives were so stark. He would see perfectly again. Or he had lost his sight for good. Tania wondered just how much strength she would have if faced with the same situation. But not once did Jonathan complain.

She read a lot to him, helped him with some of his extensive correspondence. Much of it was handled by a secretary at the hospital, but the more personal letters they now handled together. She had once taken a typing course and could type as fast as many secretaries. That delighted Jonathan. 'You could be my girl Friday,' he told her. 'Want a job in future?'

But she didn't want to think about the future. She was having enough trouble dealing with the present.

He phoned the organisers of the conference, who were incredibly efficient. There would be no trouble finding another room for Tania, a driver would meet them at the airport and then be at their disposal. 'I love working with the Americans,' Jonathan said. 'They see problems as a challenge to be overcome. Nothing is too difficult for them.'

So Tania found herself looking forward to the trip. At first the very idea of going to an unknown foreign country in charge of a newly blind man had horrified her. But now Jonathan's calm certainty made her think that this wouldn't be a problem. She was going to enjoy herself. And she would be with him.

Most of her evenings were spent alone with Jonathan. Marianne seemed to be spending a lot of the evenings with Charles, both Jonathan and Tania thought it was rather nice. One night Joe came to take Jonathan to the hospital for a meeting, and Marianne decided to stay in. 'We can have a girls' evening,' she said. 'We'll open a bottle of his wine while he's out.'

'I hope you don't think I'm deserting him at night,' she told Tania. 'I'd spend every minute of every day with him, but I think he's probably better off with just you. When we're together I want to do everything for him. I know it's not good, I've seen you make him do things that you could do so easily. But you want him to be independent.'

'It's my training,' Tania admitted. 'And don't think you're exceptional. We have to tell lots of relations not to do too much. And mums are the worst. After all, he's your little boy.'

'My only little boy,' said Marianne. 'And he doesn't realise it, but I know him very well. Much better than he thinks. Has he ever mentioned his father to you?'

The abrupt question surprised Tania. 'Hardly at all. I told him my father died young so I never knew him but that I had a wonderfully happy upbringing with my mother. He said he had been the same.'

'That's good to hear. Though it was true.' Marianne sipped from her wine, staring out of the window at the distant dark sea. 'I loved his father. We had a whirl-wind courtship in the Bahamas when I was on a pho-tographic shoot there. We were going to be married. Then he died in an accident—a silly one, falling down into the hold of a ship we were using as a background.

Of course I was terribly upset. I thought I wouldn't be able to cope. But then, two days later, things got even worse. His wife arrived—complete with two-year-old baby girl. He'd never told me he was married. I'd been betrayed.'

'And then you found out you were pregnant?' Tania guessed.

'I was pregnant. It was the late 1960s, so there was no shame attached and I was quite well-to-do. Lots of my friends were having babies without husbands—babies were fashion accessories. But I would have liked to have been married.'

'You brought up Jonathan to be a wonderful son anyway,' Tania said gently, 'and look at how he loves you now.'

'Yes, I know.' Marianne took out a handkerchief, dabbed at her eyes. 'There's a point to all this dragging up of old stories, Tania. It's to do with Jonathan.'

Tania leaned over, filled Marianne's glass. This was fascinating her.

Marianne went on, 'When he was twenty-one I told Jonathan what I have just told you, though I didn't use the word "betrayed". I said that if he wanted, I would give him the man's name. He could make enquiries, perhaps talk to people who had known his father. He might get to feel some kind of identity with him. Jonathan said he didn't want to know the man's name. The man had deceived me, he was better forgotten.'

'And he's never asked you since—shown no curiosity, no wish to know a name?'

'None. When Jonathan makes up his mind about something, that's it. He wanted to be a doctor—he worked till he became one. He wanted to become a consultant—now he is. He's incredibly determined.'

'I've noticed,' Tania said with feeling. 'You know he's now more advanced than some of my clients who have been blind for over a year. He determined to learn. He's the toughest man I've ever had to deal with.'

His mother was quiet for a moment. 'But the uncertainty is getting to him now, isn't it?' she asked. 'He's not as lively as he used to be.'

'It would get to anyone,' Tania said.

She worked, she came back to the flat at night and read to him, she made him practise his long-cane work. And in no time it was the night before they were to travel.

'Never been to America? You're going to enjoy it. And if you think it's hot here, wait till you get to Florida. It's warm and it's sticky. Not that you'll spend too much time outside. Everywhere—airport, car, hotel, conference hall—will be air-conditioned. In fact, it's a good idea to carry a light sweater or something with you. Moving from the heat outside to the chill inside can be quite traumatic.'

'I've got every woman's problem,' Tania said. 'What shall I wear?''

Marianne smiled. 'Dress casually. Just take shorts, T-shirts and a couple of light dresses. Now, we're much of a size. Can I lend you anything? I've got cases full of clothes that I very rarely wear—it goes with the job. Be good for them to have an outing.'

'We-ell,' said Tania, 'I've been thinking about when I have to stand up and give this talk. I need to have something formal, I suppose, but I don't want to look frumpy. And I'm just not sure what to choose.'

'Got just the thing,' said Marianne.

She fetched a grey dress in the finest of clinging

wools, cut absolutely simply. Tania went to try it on and found the cut worked marvels for her figure. 'I've never seen a dress that reveals so little and suggests so much,' Marianne said, pulling the skirt straight. 'Now, you need one last touch—a scarf round the neck?'

Tania had a rich red silk one. She put it on and the effect was marvellous.

'She's going to ruin your talk,' Marianne said cheerfully to her son. 'One look at Tania here and they won't listen to a word.'

'Great. That means I'll be invited back some other time. Let me feel this material, Tania.' He ran his hand down her arm. 'That feels good.'

It felt good to her, too. She loved it when he touched her.

Marianne was totally non-possessive about her clothes—they were the tools that she used in her job. She told Tania that the other models she worked with constantly borrowed from each other. It was the way they worked. So she was more than happy to lend Tania something else. Tania borrowed another two dresses—light, summer ones, but quite different from her own style.

They then all went into Jonathan's bedroom. 'While you're away, Tania's going to be your gentleman's gentleman,' Marianne said flatly. 'She'll be in charge of your clothing and there'll be no Joe there to help you dress. You're not going to embarrass her by being awkward, are you?'

Jonathan smiled and said to Tania, 'This is the woman that used to change my nappies. She's taken advantage of that fact ever since. No, I'll happily accept Tania's help.'

But Tania thought that there was just an element of

strain in his voice and she felt for him. Yet another little thing that he could no longer do for himself.

They picked the outfits that he was to wear and then Marianne packed them, with a speed and skill that amazed Tania. There was something curiously intimate about setting out his clothes, picking socks, handker-chiefs, underwear. She liked it. It was as if they... She wouldn't think that way.

'Want a hand with your packing, Tania?' Marianne asked, and she accepted. It was always good to learn from an expert.

Eventually the two cases were packed and left in the hall, the hand-baggage put nearby. The three of them sat and checked the important documents—passports, insurance, the thick pack of instructions sent to Jonathan by the conference organisers. There were Jonathan's credit cards, a sheaf of American paper money, a handful of loose change. They had talked about it, and Tania was to look after it all. She had a bag that fitted over her shoulder and under her loose sweater she would carry a money belt.

Once again Marianne gave her son a stern warning. 'Don't let it worry you that Tania's doing all the or-ganising. All the best people need help to deal with their personal affairs.'

'All right, I'm going up in the world. Look, Mum, I'm really happy that Tania's coming, and I'm grateful, too. We'll be a great team. Won't we, Tania?'

'We'll work well together,' she said. She wondered what she really meant by that.

Joe called next morning to drive them to Manchester airport. Special arrangements had been made because Jonathan was blind, and they were whisked quickly through into the final departure lounge. Tania found him a seat, then fetched them both a coffee. And she watched the great planes surge into the air, heard the distant scream of their engines.

'You're excited,' he said. 'I can tell. Why don't you go for a wander round? I always used to.'

'No,' she said, 'I'll sit here with you.' On impulse she leaned over and kissed him on the cheek. 'Thank you so much for bringing me. I'm really looking forward to it.'

He said nothing, but felt for her hand and squeezed it.

Then they were invited to board. They were in the forward cabin, the luxury club-class seats. There was a lot of leg room, the seats very wide. Much more comfortable than when she had flown previously. Though she had enjoyed that, too.

Tania had to do something so she occupied herself by keeping up a low-voiced commentary on what was happening. Jonathan had invited her to go with him so she would be his eyes. They were offered a drink—she had never had champagne at this hour of the morning before. Then there were the usual announcements, the taxiing, the jerk as the plane drove forward and the bumpy ride that eased the moment they were airborne.

'If you don't mind, I think I'll sleep,' he said. 'All doctors learn to sleep, anywhere, anytime.'

But Tania couldn't sleep during the day, so she went over his speech again, and then the stewardess found her a couple of glossy magazines.

She woke him when it was time for the meal, and they had a glass of red wine each. Afterwards she found herself dozing, perhaps the effect of the alcohol. And Jonathan went to sleep again.

It happened quite a while afterwards. She vaguely realised there was some kind of commotion in the economy section, and a couple of stewards rushed through the curtain that separated the two sections. Shortly afterwards, those fateful words came through on the intercom. 'Is there a doctor on board?' Beside her she felt Jonathan awake instantly.

'Ask a steward if there is a doctor on board,' he said, 'and if there isn't get someone to come and tell me exactly what has happened.'

She did as he suggested. There wasn't a doctor available, and two minutes later an apprehensive steward was telling him what had happened. An old gentleman in an aisle seat had suddenly collapsed. It had been impossible to wake him and the cabin crew had half dragged, half carried him to the kitchen where he could be laid flat. They couldn't find a pulse.

'Lead us to him,' Jonathan said. 'You've got a blind doctor and two-thirds of a nurse. And fetch whatever medical kit you have. Tania, you come, too.'

They were led promptly down one of the aisles, the rest of the passengers remaining apprehensively in their seats. Tania guided Jonathan so he was kneeling by the man, feeling at his chest. There was little pulse. Tania pulled aside the man's clothes while a steward found a stethoscope for Jonathan. Jonathan listened to the chest, grunted. 'Thought so—cardiac arrest. Go and tell the captain we should divert to the nearest airport. Have an ambulance waiting with resuscitation equipment aboard. Now, don't all planes carry a defibrillator these days?'

'It's here,' one of the cabin crew said, 'but there's no one on board who's been trained to use it. The girl who was trained had her shift changed.'

'Remarkable,' Jonathan said. 'Put it in front of me anyway. Tania, describe what you see. And then check the man's chest again, see if there's a scar suggesting he might have been fitted with a pacemaker.'

There was no pacemaker scar. She had assisted with defibrillation before, but had never even seen one of these new portable machines. It was an SAD—a semi-automatic defibrillator. She told Jonathan what she saw, followed his instructions and attached two electrodes to the patient's chest. They moved back, waited for the machine to assess the patient. Then a suitable shock size flashed into the screen. 'Let's try it,' said Jonathan after she had read out what was there.

They—or the patient—were in luck. The heart re-started at once. Jonathan told her to draw up morphine and inject it, told the stewards to fit the man with an oxygen mask and give him as much as was possible. Then they remained watching for another ten minutes.

'The nearest airport is still Orlando,' a steward told them. 'We've radioed for clearance and the ambulance.'

'Then all we can do is hope. We'll go back to our seats. Fetch us if there's any change.'

They sat back in their seats together and agreed that, yes, they would both like another drink. Jonathan asked for a brandy and Tania decided to join him. She had found the past half-hour more stressful than anything in a long time.

'You know, I think you enjoyed that,' she whispered to him after they had accepted their drinks. 'You were sorry for the man, of course, but you enjoyed it.'

'I'm afraid I did a little. Didn't you enjoy it as well?'

She couldn't understand how he could be so calm.

'I was terrified! I don't care if I did train as a nurse for two years, I was still terrified.'

'We both did some good,' he said, 'and it made me feel useful for a change. How does it feel to know that you just probably saved someone's life?'

'I didn't! You did.'

'You know very well that I couldn't have managed without you. Now, how does it feel?'

She thought for a minute. What he'd said was true—he probably couldn't have managed without her. So how did she feel? 'It feels good,' she said.

They were now flying in sight of the coast of America. Tania stared, entranced, out of the window. The coastline was so vast, there were so few signs of civilisation compared with England. Then there was the brilliant greenness of Florida, with its scattering of tiny lakes. And then they landed.

An ambulance was waiting. Paramedics hustled on board and carried off their patient. 'He stands a chance now,' said Jonathan. 'Hope he makes it.'

Then the passengers were allowed to disembark. Once again they were escorted through customs and immigration. Their bags were retrieved for them, placed on a trolley. And as they moved into the open concourse, there waiting for them was an enormous, earnest-looking young man. He held a sign saying DR KNIGHT, but he recognised them at once.

'Good afternoon, Miss Richardson, Dr Knight. I'm Pierce Hardy, I've been assigned to you during your stay. May I show you my identity?' On a chain round his neck was a card holding his name and photograph, with a stamped statement saying that he was an ac-credited member of the conference.

After Tania had inspected it he solemnly shook

hands with them both and then took charge of the luggage trolley. 'I have a car waiting outside. Please, ask me anything, I'll help if I can. Our aim is to make sure your stay is useful, profitable and comfortable. Now, shall we go to your hotel first?'

Tania had her first taste of Florida weather as she walked from the airport to the car. It was worse than she had expected—hot and sticky, as Jonathan had said. But the car had its engine running and was cool inside.

'Normally secretaries are in a separate block, but I understand that you have adjoining rooms so you can be of extra assistance to Dr Knight?' Pierce asked her.

'That's right,' Tania said, trying not to giggle.

'It must be a terrible thing, sir, an accident such as yours,' Pierce said to Jonathan. 'When I heard about it I read up on it at once. Terrible but fascinating.'

'You're a medical student, Pierce?'

'In my third year, sir. I hope to learn a lot from this conference.'

'I hope you do, too.' Jonathan seemed to accept Pierce's presence as entirely normal. 'What's the programme for the rest of the day, Pierce?'

'Well, I'm at your disposal if you want to go anywhere, see anything. Or if you need anything I'll try to get it for you. But the first official function is the reception at the conference centre at 7.30 this evening. Usually black tie, sir.'

'You can pick us up at seven, then. We won't be going out again this afternoon.'

The hotel was white-painted, luxurious. Pierce arranged the transfer of the luggage, took Tania to the desk to sign in and accompanied them to the fifth floor to make sure all was well. Then, when he was abso-

lutely sure that there was nothing more he could possibly do, he left them. He would meet them in the foyer
at seven that night.

'Sit there while I have a quick look round,' she said
to Jonathan, 'then I'll come back and tell you about
the place.' They had adjoining rooms—adjoining
suites, in effect. Each suite had a bedroom with a bathroom opening off it, and a slightly larger living room.
The two living rooms had the connecting door. It
couldn't have been better arranged. His case was in one
bedroom, hers was in the other. She came back into
his sitting room, sat opposite him and giggled.

'I like it when you laugh like that,' he said. 'What
especially are you thinking of?'

'I was thinking of Pierce. A very proper, very earnest
young man. He went to such trouble to indicate that he
knew we had adjoining rooms because I needed to help
you. We mustn't think that he thought that we were—'

'Of course not,' said Jonathan. 'The very idea! And
we're not, are we? Not yet anyway. But when—and
if—I get my sight back, we'll pay the place a return
visit.'

She noticed that, as ever, he hadn't said *when* he
regained his sight. The 'if' was always there. As if he
was preparing himself for possible disappointment.

'Tell me about the room,' Jonathan said. 'Is there
any chance of me falling off the balcony?'

There was a balcony and they were on the fifth floor.
Instantly she was alarmed. 'Jonathan! You do *not* go
on that balcony unless I'm with you. Understand?
There's a high railing, of course, but you do *not* go out
there.'

'OK, I won't,' he murmured. 'Especially if I have
large amounts to drink.'

She knew there was no danger of that. But there had been cases of newly blind people drinking to excess, perhaps to drown their sorrows, and then having the most appalling accidents. Especially falls. It didn't bear thinking about.

'Sorry,' she said. 'I didn't mean to shout. Come on, we'll learn to trail the place.'

He needed to be as independent as possible. He learned to navigate the bathroom, the bed, found the telephone, managed to master the control panel that turned on the television and radio channels. 'Shan't be paying much attention to those,' he said. He learned to cope with the air-conditioning unit. Then he wandered round the sitting room, touching the chairs and the rest of the furniture.

'There's a packet of information here,' she said. 'Let me read odd bits to you.' Then she unpacked for him, even though she knew he didn't want her to.

'Now, go to your own room for a while,' he ordered when she'd finished. 'Come back in, say, an hour. Have a shower or a bath, but I suggest you don't sleep. You're to enjoy this, too. I won't have you running round after me all the time.'

'It's not running round after you. It's what I'm here for and I like it!'

'Just do as you're told.' He grinned.

In fact, it was a good idea to leave him alone for a while. He had to acclimatise to things in his own way. This was the first time he had ever stayed anywhere but in his own flat since he'd been blinded. He needed to get used to the strangeness of it.

When Tania went back to Jonathan's room later—carefully knocking first—she found that he had also showered and had changed into fresh T-shirt and chinos. His hair was still damp, his eyes bright. He looked healthy and fit and... He just looked wonderful.

'There's a mini-bar somewhere,' he told her. 'Why don't you find it then look to see if there's any freshly squeezed orange juice? There usually is in these places and it's always wonderful.'

She found the bar and the juice, poured them a glass each. Yes, it *was* wonderful. Then, again at his suggestion, she led him very carefully out onto the balcony. She settled him in one of the two chairs before seating herself. 'It's warm,' she said. But there was a bit of a breeze, and it was pleasant to sit in the sun.

'I'm enjoying myself,' he said, 'and that's entirely due to you.'

'No. It's due to the conference organisers and to Pierce. They're the ones who are looking after you.'

He shook his head. 'They make this trip possible. You make it pleasant. I could cope without you—possibly. But with you I can have a good time. I like your company, Tania.'

'I'm enjoying myself, too,' she pointed out. But his compliment had warmed her.

He suggested that they order something light to eat from room service. 'Pick something out of the menu,' he suggested. So she found the menu—long and fascinating—and read it out to him. Then at his insistence, she picked something first. Something typically American. A swordfish steak sandwich with a side order of salad and shrimps with Marie-Rose sauce?

'Sounds good,' he said, 'and I'll ask for coffee for two as well.'

'But what do you want?'

'I'm going to share yours. Don't worry, I've had

sandwiches from here before. There'll be enough for two.'

She didn't believe him until the waiter turned up with his little trolley and laid the sandwich out on the table on the balcony. 'I guess you're right,' she said.

After a while she insisted that Jonathan listen while she read the speech to him again. By now she almost knew most of it, and he could tell her which passages to read more slowly, which sections to emphasize. 'You've got a good reading voice,' he said eventually. 'Have you ever thought of volunteering to record things? You could start with non-fiction, then perhaps move on to short stories and novels.'

She had told him about the variety of reading material that was recorded for blind people. 'No, I've never thought of recording myself,' she said. 'I'm glad that you think I could do it.'

'You know that I think that you're beautiful? People have told me so, but I knew it anyway. Well, your voice is part of your beauty.'

Tania didn't know what to say. When he talked about her being beautiful, she always felt like a cheat. 'Perhaps it's time we went to get changed,' she said. But she knew he had noticed how she hadn't replied to his compliment.

The reception that evening was to be formal. Jonathan said he'd take no time to put on his dinner jacket, but she would need far longer. So she went back to her room to change. She had brought her new wonderful dress with her—but she was saving it for the big ball on the last night. Tonight she would wear a pink cotton dress she'd borrowed from Marianne. It was just sufficiently formal. She brushed her hair, saw to her make-up. Perhaps Jonathan wouldn't see her but his friends would, and she didn't want to let him down.

When she knocked and went back into his room she found him considerably irritated. He was in shirtsleeves and trousers, his jacket lying on the bed. And in his hand was his black bow-tie. 'Can you tie this?' he asked. 'Usually I'm an expert, but I now realise I must have a mirror to help me. Joe did it for me last time.'

'You could send down for a ready-tied one,' she suggested.

He looked horrified. 'Never! I'd be known ever after as the consultant with the made-up tie. I've got to do this somehow.'

'Well, I've never done one before,' she said, 'but I'll try. Tell me how to do it.'

She stood facing him and tried to follow his instructions. It was no good. 'We're facing different ways,' she said, 'and you can't get your mind round it. I'm going to stand behind you. But you'll have to sit down.'

So Jonathan sat on the dressing-table stool, she knelt behind him, reached over his shoulders and followed his instructions. That was much easier. She could see the tie coming together in the mirror.

But it was an odd position. She had to press close to him. In the very flimsy bra that Marianne had made her buy, her breasts were obvious. She could feel the warmth of his body through the thin cotton of her dress. She wondered—and it made the situation worse—if he could feel her nipples coming erect because of the pressure. But he said nothing.

Finally the tie was tied, and Tania sighed with relief. 'It's done,' she said. 'Perhaps not as well as you'd do it, but there's no reason to be ashamed of it.'

He touched the bow-tie, nodded approvingly. 'I'm glad you've finished. Having your body so close to mine was…having an effect on me.'

'Put your jacket on,' she said, blushing.

She checked his hair, tugged at the jacket, brushed it down. Both of them put on the rather large badges they had been issued, giving their names, titles, hospitals and so on. 'You're going to be a credit to me,' she said.

'I hope I will but I think all eyes will be on you. I need something to dream about. What are you wearing?'

She told him, describing his mother's dress. 'May I…feel?' he asked.

'Yes, you may if you wish, but don't mess my make-up.' She tried to keep the tremor from her voice.

As he had done before, he touched her face, very delicately. He ran his fingers down her neck, her arms, across to her waist. Then he hesitated. 'Go on,' she said. 'I don't mind. I told you before, I rather like it.'

So he let his fingers stray gently over her breasts, and she thought she found it as exciting as he obviously did. Unable to stop herself, she bent forward and gave him a quick kiss. 'Soon be time to meet Pierce,' she said. 'Just one more thing—you're to wear dark glasses.' She handed them to him.

'I'll feel like an American gangster in these,' he grumbled.

'It's a courtesy to other people as much as anything,' she said.

Reluctantly, he had to agree. He wore the glasses as a sign that he was blind. If people didn't realise this, he might unwittingly offend someone.

Pierce was on time to the second. 'I took a liberty,

Dr Knight,' he said. 'I understand that your…ocular deficiency is quite recent, so I asked the chef to prepare suitable food.'

'I'm impressed,' Jonathan said gravely. 'Any student with such an attention to detail will make an excellent doctor.'

Pierce blushed. 'Thank you, sir,' he said. 'If you'll just wait here, I'll fetch the car.'

'Aren't you impressed, Tania?' Jonathan asked when he was sure Pierce was out of earshot.

'I'm impressed with anyone who can say "ocular deficiency" and not smile,' she said.

They drove through busy streets in the air-conditioned car. When they stopped at the lights Tania was amused by the voices she could hear. Most of them were British. Still, this was obviously a foreign country. The iced-cake architecture suggested this.

The conference centre was enormous! She had been to one or two conferences when she'd been training, but never to anywhere like this. It was a set of domes in white concrete, surrounded by acres of bright green grass.

Pierce drove them to the entrance, saw them out of the car and handed them over to someone else who was waiting for them. When they wished to leave, they were to say so at the main desk, and three minutes later Pierce would pick them up.

'I've never been treated as efficiently as this before,' she muttered to Jonathan.

'The American way,' he said. 'They're brilliant at detail.'

They were led to the foyer, Tania describing what they were passing. Jonathan had been here before and knew what to expect. The room was large and people stood around in small groups, talking. A waiter hovered with a tray, offering them a choice of water, orange juice or California champagne. She took champagne for them both.

'I hope I haven't ignored someone I know,' he whispered to her. 'I guess I'll just have to beam at the world in general.'

'You're not a generally beaming type. I think you're—'

'Jonathan!' A tall, broad man with a Texan accent and a bootlace tie, instead of the normal black bow-tie, stood smiling in front of them. 'Jonathan, it's good to see you. Sorry to hear about your accident. Matt McKie here.'

'No one could mistake that accent, Matt. Good to…say hello again.' They shook hands and Jonathan went on, 'I'd like to introduce my good friend, Tania Richardson, who's acting as my eyes.'

'Good to see you, too, Tania.' Her hand was taken and gently squeezed. 'And this is my wife, Glenys.' Matt went on, 'I've asked for us to be together at dinner, Jonathan. Now, I want you to tell me all about the prognosis for your oncoming operation. And while we have a minute, I've got a couple of fellows very interested in your theories on treating TB in Africa.' He turned again to Tania. 'You don't mind if I borrow him a minute, do you, Tania?'

Glenys said, 'I'll look after Tania for a while.' When the two men had gone, she went on, 'You've heard of golf widows? Well, conference widows are worse off. Is this your first time here?'

'I'm afraid it is,' said Tania, 'I'm just getting used to things.'

'Then let me tell you all about the shops,' Glenys said.

'How do you feel?' Jonathan asked. 'You've had a long day. And looking after me must make you even more tired.'

'It was a lot easier than I thought,' Tania admitted, 'though I am flagging a bit now. Wasn't everyone kind?'

'They're like that. How much did you manage to write down?'

'More than a little. I'll decipher it all and read it back to you tomorrow.'

It had been her idea to take a small notebook and pen to jot down all the notes, telephone numbers, addresses that had been offered to Jonathan. It had been a good idea.

She looked around. 'You know, there's a kettle on a tray over there. Want a cup of tea?'

'This evening I've drunk champagne, red wine, water and extra-strong coffee. A cup of tea sounds perfect.'

They were back in his room. The reception hadn't gone on too late. Jonathan said that everyone would be up early next morning. She filled the kettle, then went to her own room to fetch a packet of Assam teabags. Marianne had told her to bring them.

He took off his jacket and tie and sighed as he sipped his tea. 'Look out of the window,' he told her. 'I remember the view from here. At night the lights are quite something.'

She did as he suggested. He was right, the lights were wondrous. Just for a moment she realised what he was missing and felt a pang of sadness for him. But she said nothing. 'How did it go for you?' she asked.

'Well. But I'm tired now. It's interesting. Being blind means that you miss a lot but that there's also a lot that you pick up. The couple opposite us at dinner—the Trentons. Are they having a bad time? With their marriage I mean?'

She looked at him in amazement. 'I thought they were ideally happy,' she said. 'They certainly acted that way. But then I saw—just once when he was talking to the woman on his other side, with his back to his wife—I saw she looked at him with—disappointment? But only once. How did you pick up on it?'

He shrugged. 'If you miss body language you pick up on intonation. In future I'm going to tell my students to try listening with their eyes shut. Surprising what you can find out. That is, if I ever have any more students.'

'Jonathan! That's the first time I've heard you sound sorry for yourself.'

'Not sorry,' he said, 'just realistic. Now, time for bed.' He frowned as he heard her take his jacket and tie and put them away. 'I really don't like you acting as my maid, Tania.'

'And I don't mind in the least. It's nothing to some of the jobs I've had to do in the past. Now, I'm going to leave your bedroom door, my bedroom door and the other two doors between us all open. This is a new environment for you, you might get disorientated. Any problem, call me.'

'So I could just get out of my bed and walk straight to yours?'

'You could. But I know you won't. Goodnight.' She kissed him lightly on the lips.

She cleansed her face, showered and slipped on her nightie. Then she listened at the door of his darkened room and heard the sound of heavy breathing. He was asleep. She now realised how tremendously tired she was herself. But when she slipped into bed, it was some time before she herself slept.

Next day was half frightening, half exciting. They ordered a light breakfast in Jonathan's room and ate it outside on the balcony in their dressing-gowns. Already it was hot. Then he put on a lightweight fawn suit and she put on a light blue dress, another one she'd borrowed from Marianne.

Pierce was waiting for them, anxious to know whether they'd had a good night. And then it was back to the conference centre—now to be used as just that.

This morning they were to be in a vast auditorium. Pierce stayed with them this time, taking them to an antechamber where they were fitted with lapel microphones and shown how to turn them on and off. Then they were escorted to seats in the very front row. There was a great pack of written material which Pierce said he would keep for them.

The conference was on the spread and control of infectious diseases. Tania had some medical knowledge but much of what was said was above her head. However, what she did understand was fascinating. There were two main themes. The first was that with improved communications, with so many people travelling the world, diseases once thought to be eradicated were now coming back to the West from the Third World. The second was that if antibiotics continued to be used as freely as at present, they might become ineffective. They were both sobering ideas.

Each speaker was introduced by the chairman, talked for about thirty minutes and then answered questions from the floor, the questions being picked by the chairman.

'How're you enjoying it so far?' Jonathan asked her after a while.

'I'm impressed but I'm still nervous,' she whispered back. 'When are we on?'

'We're the second talk this afternoon. Don't worry, you'll be all right. I can sense what people are thinking—they're interested. So they'll be interested in us.'

They had the lightest of lunches, a sandwich with Matt McKie who came looking for them, then back to their seats, the lunch-break having been very short.

Tania couldn't concentrate on the first talk, she was too nervous, though she saw that Jonathan was intent. Then it was their turn.

The chairman stood and called Jonathan. Trembling, Tania helped him up onto the stage. There was a chair for him by her side and the chairman helped him to it. She stood behind the lectern, opened her folder and looked at row upon row of faces in front of her. What was she doing here? She was terrified! But then she thought of Jonathan in his new world of darkness, and decided that if he could cope with good grace, so could she.

The chairman introduced Jonathan and explained his loss of sight. There was a spontaneous round of applause at this. Then it was her turn. She turned on her microphone and started speaking. Her words echoed round the chamber most satisfactorily. After that it was easy. Her rehearsals hadn't been in vain.

At the end of her speech she was thanked by the chairman and applauded by the audience. She took the chair offered to her and Jonathan rose to answer questions. Again, very satisfactory. When the chairman declared the section at an end she let Jonathan take her arm and escorted him from the stage. They were applauded again.

'You did very well,' he whispered to her when they were sitting again.

'You mean you did very well,' she whispered back.

Next day was something quite different. Tables were set all the way round the main foyer. Behind each sat one of the previous day's speakers. There were also a few people with tables who hadn't spoken but would speak the next day.

Pierce led them to their table. He also provided them with a large sign giving Jonathan's name, his qualifications and his publications. There were also piles of papers which Jonathan had written and the organisers had printed.

Delegates were invited to walk round, to sit and talk to whoever they wanted. 'If no one calls, pretend you don't care,' he told her. 'But in general the size of your queue represents your importance. Lecturers have been known to bribe people to come and ask questions just so they'll look busy and important.'

'Just like a dance I once went to,' she murmured, 'but I don't think it's going to be your problem.' A queue was already forming at Jonathan's station.

In fact, he got a large number of visitors. And they weren't really interested in his blindness—in fact, Tania suspected that one or two of them didn't actually realise Jonathan was blind. They were more interested in what he had to say.

She was kept busy, too. Many of the delegates left

papers of their own, as well as addresses and telephone numbers for Jonathan to call in the future. Organising this material was her responsibility, and her folder and notebook got fuller and fuller, but she enjoyed it.

Pierce hovered ever near, keeping the iced-water carafe filled, fetching them coffee, orange juice and sandwiches. Red with embarrassment, he asked if Jonathan wished to visit the 'comfort station'. Breezily, Jonathan agreed. Then he returned to carry on with his work.

It was a full day and it went on until late. Eventually they were driven back to the hotel, where they would have a meal in their room.

'Tired?' he asked her.

'I'm worn out! And you must be near collapse. How you keep this up for days on end I don't know.'

'I quite enjoy it. But we'll have an early night.'

Tania really enjoyed their evening meal together. At Jonathan's suggestion she asked for the seafood platter and salad. It was wonderful! There were tidbits there that she didn't recognise and some she did recognise but wasn't too sure about. But it was all delicious. And the salad? 'I'm going to start making salad with a blue cheese dressing,' she told him.

When they had finished and the waiter had taken the dishes, he put a scarlet, paper-wrapped package on the table in front of her. 'I'm not going to the conference tomorrow,' he said. 'Instead, I'm staying here in the morning and I've arranged for three or four people to come to see me in my room. It'll be more private, we'll get more done. I want you to go shopping with Pierce.'

'Shopping? But don't you need me here?'

'Not with these people. There'll be no notes for you to take, and you'll only be bored. Besides, wouldn't you like to go shopping?'

'I'd love to,' she said, 'but I came here to help you and—'

'It's decided,' he said. 'Pierce knows where to take you. You go to a mall and enjoy yourself.'

'What about the afternoon?'

'In the afternoon I thought we'd be real tourists. You've seen the pool here?'

Indeed she had—a great expanse of blue water, shaded by palm trees and with loungers lying round it. There was a chute for the children, Jacuzzis, a waterfall and a fountain. There was also a wave section. There were bars at each end and even a bar that served you as you stood in the water. 'It's different from the corporation baths where I learned to swim,' she said.

'I can believe it. I thought we might spend a couple of hours there, just relaxing. It's quiet, you can take me for a swim. And I've been a bit forward. As a tiny thank-you present I bought you this. Well, I got Pierce to buy it for you. I thought you might like to wear it.'

He pushed the packet over to her. Not knowing what to expect, but excited anyway, she tore open the scarlet paper. There, wrapped carefully in tissue paper, was— a bikini. It was dark blue. A detached onlooker would have thought it would go well with her hair.

But Tania wasn't detached. She looked at the little scraps of material in dismay. There was no way she would allow herself to be seen in this. The scarring on her abdomen…it would show it all!

'You don't like it,' he said quietly. 'I've picked the wrong thing.'

'No, no, it's lovely,' she said. 'And, Jonathan, it's so good of you to think of me. But…but I never wear a bikini. I've got a one-piece costume, that's all I ever wear. I know it sounds strange, but I just don't like two-pieces. It's one of my peculiarities. Please, forgive me. It's a lovely thought and a lovely present.'

'We're all entitled to a few peculiarities,' he said. 'Tomorrow you can get Pierce to take you back to the shop, see if you can change this for a style you like. But it'll still be dark blue, won't it?'

'Oh, yes,' she said, 'it'll still be dark blue. Jonathan, please don't be cross with me.'

'Who could be cross with you?' he asked.

She thought there was a thoughtfulness in his voice that she didn't much care for. Had she given anything away?

CHAPTER NINE

IT HAD only been four days since they'd returned, but the conference now seemed long ago. Back in England, the weather was still hot but after Florida it didn't seem too bad. Tania had enjoyed herself thoroughly—it had been an interesting interlude in her life. But now she was home, and things were going to change.

She had seen a different side to Jonathan, thought so much more of him. She had seen the professional side of his life. But the most interesting thing about it was how many friends he had. Jonathan was popular. People liked him, not only as a doctor but as a friend. She thought that was wonderful, but it made the next few days so much harder to bear.

In Florida she had kept the door between their suites open all the time. It had been so hard not to get out of her bed and go to his—but she had resisted the temptation. She guessed he felt the same way. But never had he pressured her, even told her what he wanted. Jonathan was a gentleman.

Now they were back at his flat. Everyone tried to keep up the appearance of normality but they all knew that soon things would be vitally different. Marianne was still there, Joe called every day, Eleanor called often, Jerry O'Connor called, Charles called. All of them were under a strain.

Jonathan seemed to be the toughest of them all. But one night, when his mother had left to cry in her bedroom, it was a sign of the strain he was under when he said, with great good temper, 'You're a gloomy lot. I'm the one who's supposed to be suffering.'

'It'll all be over soon,' Tania said. 'When we know, things will be different. It's waiting that hurts.'

She was still on holiday, but she called in at work. Derrick, as stiff as ever, told her that her temporary job would soon disappear, they were definitely appointing a full-time worker. But she was welcome to apply and he would certainly give her a good reference. She took the application form and said nothing.

It was the night before Jonathan went into hospital. Tania told Marianne to go out for the evening with Charles and spend the night at his house. With unusual frankness, she said, 'You can't help but be miserable. That'll only make him feel the same way. You go out and I'll try to cheer us both up.'

'I wish I was tough like him,' Marianne said, 'but I'm not.' She agreed to go.

Tania had her own plans for the evening. She asked Joe to come round early on to take Jonathan for a run on the sands. Then she cooked them a meal and they sat together in the window, eating and chatting and listening to music. And quite early, she told him, 'I'm coming to your bed tonight, Jonathan.'

She turned off the light, they were both in complete darkness. She told him that he must hold her, that his arms must be round her all the time. He could kiss her lips, her breasts, but nowhere else. And he must hold her all the time.

They made love slowly at first, as if each wanted to prolong it as long as possible. This was so different from the wild, animal-like act in the garden. And she kissed his body, it seemed to be what he wanted.

Then they were joined in the final ecstatic excitement, and she felt her love for him flower as she opened her body to him, heard the hoarseness of his frenzied cry. And then they lay there, their sweat-slicked bodies side by side. She lay on her front so his casually stroking hand couldn't touch her where she didn't want it to.

Jonathan's hands touched her face, felt her tears. 'There's no need to cry for me, Tania,' he said softly. 'If we have this, then we have everything.'

It was a natural mistake to make but she wasn't crying for him—but for herself, or for them both. Desperately, she wanted him to regain his sight. But if he did...then she would never see him again. No way was he to see her scarred body. He would be repelled.

Jonathan thought he loved her. But he was a lover of beauty—and she couldn't face seeing his disappointment in her.

The next evening he was to go into hospital for prepping. He would be operated on first thing the morning after that, but Charles didn't want any visitors there until after the operation was complete. 'I need to concentrate,' he growled, 'and you'd only put me off.'

So Tania saw Jonathan for the last time the evening before the operation. She could kiss him, of course, but it was different from when they were alone together. He was in hospital now and she felt that the operation had already begun.

'Just one thing,' he said. 'When I go under the anaesthetic I'll be thinking of you. And that beautiful, beautiful body.'

'And I'll be thinking of you,' she said.

*   *   *

'How d'you feel?' Charles asked. It was late at night and his old friend had just called in to see Jonathan before he had the sedative that would be necessary to make him sleep.

'Quite calm,' Jonathan said steadily. 'One thing about being blind—you get a lot of chances to think about things. And whatever happens in the operation tomorrow, I know I've got good things to look forward to.'

'You mean Tania?'

'Yes, I do. It was worth having this accident just to meet her.' He ignored Charles's grunt of disapproval and went on, 'Now there's something I want. My neurosurgery is a bit rusty. I want you to go through in detail what you'll be doing tomorrow. If I know what's happening, I'll be happier.'

For a moment Charles was silent. Then he said, 'Well, you are a doctor. I'll tell you what I propose. You'll be anaesthetised, brought into the theatre and strapped to a chair. I'll sit behind you. We'll cut through the skull, get into the occipital lobe. I'm hoping to find some cause of pressure and to relieve it. Scans show there is something there. But all we can do is hope. You happier now?'

'Reasonably. You can send that nurse down now who's going to give me something to help me sleep. And get a good night's sleep yourself. I need you alert tomorrow morning.'

'Goodnight, then, Jonathan.' Charles gripped his shoulder and was gone.

He was scared. Jonathan could admit it to himself, though he would never admit it to anyone else. Except Tania, he thought. Yes, he could admit it to her—in fact, he had already done so.

Tomorrow the operation would succeed or it wouldn't. If it did, he would resume his job, wait a few weeks and ask Tania to marry him. If the operation didn't succeed—well, he would do the same. Wait a few weeks, sort out a new life, make sure that Tania was happy and then ask her to marry him. He'd think of this as a situation in which he couldn't lose.

The sedative started to take effect, his thoughts started to blue… He'd prefer it if he regained his sight…but, whatever, he'd have Tania…

He was sitting up. He could hear vague things. Where was he…? Who was he…? He couldn't really be bothered, he'd go back to sleep. His head hurt.

A little later he went through the process again. He was sitting up. His head hurt and he… A voice said, 'Can you hear me, Jonathan? It's Charles, Charles Forsythe. I want you to try to open your eyes.'

He didn't want to open his eyes, that might make him wake up. And that was the last thing he wanted. Still, if Charles was asking… He opened his eyes.

It was queer, he'd never seen anything like it. Vision seemed to start at the outsides of his eyes then move slowly inwards. Things were blurred, but he could focus, he was getting things right. Yes, that was a ceiling. Very definitely a ceiling, painted white and with a strip light in the middle of it.

'What can you see, Jonathan?'

He turned his head, very slowly, and looked at his old friend Charles. 'Well, I can see you for a start,' he said, 'and then I guess I'm in a ward somewhere… I'm not sure that I…' Then memory came crashing back and he screamed. 'Charles! I can see!' For the first time since he was nine, tears ran down his face.

He still felt very vague, it would take hours for the anaesthetic to wear off. But there were two people who just had to see him. He kissed his mother. Then he kissed Tania—and looked at her. 'I knew you were beautiful,' he said, 'and now I can see you.'

But all Tania could do was cry. He needed to sleep again.

The next day he still had a headache but he was feeling much better. Now he could look forward to taking up his job again—it would be quite a while, but Charles had told him the operation had been a success. All now would be well. His mother came to see him, Joe came to see him, there was a line of other well-wishers wanting to see him, but the ward sister wouldn't let them in for a while. No visit from Tania. That was strange.

The day after that, apart from the large number of get-well cards, there was a letter for him, hand-delivered. 'I was told to make sure you got this in person,' the young nurse said, 'but not to give it to you till this afternoon.'

Curious, he opened it. It was from Tania. She had left him.

Once, not so long ago, Jonathan would have got instantly angry. But not this time. He was sad but more than that he was determined. Her words only told half a story. He wanted to know it all.

He phoned his mother who was both puzzled and upset. She said she had come back to the flat to find that Tania had gone, taken all her belongings with her, just left a note to say how much she'd enjoyed being Marianne's friend.

Jonathan frowned, and waited for Joe to call to see him. Then, without comment, he showed him the note.

'I don't believe it,' Joe said flatly. 'I suppose you want me to make a couple of enquiries?'

He came back that evening. 'Something's very wrong,' he said. 'She's given up her job. She hasn't left a forwarding address, she's told no one where she's living. She only mentioned that she might be going abroad again. Jonathan, she's just disappeared.'

'Then I'm going to make her reappear,' Jonathan said savagely.

Tania couldn't remember ever feeling so miserable, so listless. Even when she had been recovering from the burns she had never been as low as this. Everything was too much trouble; nothing was worthwhile. There was only the heartache that never left her.

Sometimes she thought about when she had been in hospital, slowly recovering from those terrible burns. This pain was worse. At least in hospital there had been something to look forward to, the belief that in time the pain would go away. She knew that this pain would never disappear.

Vaguely, she thought about her future, skimmed through papers and magazines. Perhaps she should start to train as a nurse again. She didn't think she wanted to work in a blind school again. She had done that, it was too hurtful. So she just sat, watched, sometimes walked. She was alone but not lonely

This place had always been a refuge. An old, green-painted caravan perched on the lip of a hill on a farm. It was her cousin's farm, and she had stayed there often. There were happy memories of weeks spent there with her mother, and later on she'd stayed weeks there convalescing after she'd been discharged from the hospital.

Most days she sat outside, looking into the valley below. In the valley was the town of Buxton. She could see the Crescent, the park, the Palace Hotel, the great dome of the hospital. There were people down there, she thought, with lives and ambitions and loves. Not like her. She was apart from all that.

She had money saved. If she wanted, she could stay here for weeks—months even. There was nothing to make her want to move.

Sometimes she wondered about Jonathan. She knew he'd be upset, but he'd get over it. It was in his character to fight against adversity. He'd forget her, find someone else, someone who was truly beautiful. She knew the operation would stay successful. She'd had a private word with Charles and he'd assured her that now there was nothing to worry about. But she rather missed talking to Marianne. Marianne had been a friend.

Sooner or later, she supposed, she'd have to do something. But not yet. She'd stay here in her bolt-hole until the pain healed. She'd sit here in the shade and look down on all the people rushing round in Buxton.

'Hello, Tania. It's so good to see you.' The words were soft, gentle.

Jonathan! What was he doing here? How had he found her? For a moment she just couldn't cope with the tumult of emotions that were rushing through her. There was anger, horror, pain, surprise—but above all there was love. And that made the pain greater.

She was sitting in a deckchair, looking out over the valley. He picked up another one leaning against the caravan, unfolded it and sat opposite her.

'Whatever it is, you could have told me, Tania. You said there were reasons. We could have sorted them out together.'

Then he leaned forward, took her head in his two hands, bent forward and kissed her. A soft, a loving kiss that touched her very soul. Did he know what he was doing to her? For a while she was content to stay there, ecstatically happy. Then she gently pushed him away. This couldn't go on. She just didn't know what to say or think or feel. So she took refuge in the commonplace. 'How did you find me?'

'I've been wandering round Buxton for the past two days. Remember how you once told me about having a bolt-hole—somewhere you could go to in your imagination when life got too much? You described this place. I thought it was real, so I came to look for it.'

He sighed. 'This was the last place I came to, Tania. You don't know how afraid I was that you wouldn't be here. I didn't know where else to look.'

She couldn't deal with the sadness in his voice. 'My bolt-hole,' she said. 'I remember you describing your bolt-hole—a beach with beautiful, half-clad ladies on it.'

'Just one,' he corrected her. 'A beach with one beautiful half-clad lady.'

'Whatever. I thought you might go there to recuperate.'

'Perhaps I would have. But you were the beauty I wanted to be with. Tania, why did you go? Don't you know how I feel about you?'

She couldn't stand it when he used that tone. She said, 'You were blind, you were desperate. We had a purely physical thing. It was good but now it's over. Ships that passed in the night, Jonathan.'

'It was all night to me,' he pointed out, 'but, still, I take your point. So, if it was purely physical, what about one last time? You know how I dreamed about seeing you naked—why can't I just once?'

'You're just like all men,' she screamed. 'The very idea—'

'The very idea of seeing you naked? I know, Tania. There's something you don't want me to see. You're scarred or something like that, aren't you?'

She couldn't answer. White-faced, she stared at him.

'My mother worked it out,' he said gently, 'and she told me how much it might mean to you. I told her about the bikini I bought you—and she told me that you didn't want her near when you were changing. Then I remembered, when we were making love you made me keep my arms round your neck. What didn't you want me to see or feel, Tania?'

'Every time we were together,' she said, 'you told me how much you loved beautiful women, how much you wanted to see me. See me naked, I mean. Do you know how much that hurt me?'

His face was stricken. 'Tania...I never thought. I knew you were beautiful—I wanted you to know how much I wanted you.'

'I'm only part beautiful.' She sighed. 'I'll tell you the rest and then you can go. I had an accident—I was really badly burned across my abdomen, and I spent months in the burns unit in hospital. Then I was discharged, and I started to work as a trainee nurse again. You must remember, I was very weak—emotionally weak, that is. A long stay in hospital can affect you.' She looked at him curiously. 'Of course, you know that, don't you?'

'I do,' he said.

'Well, I got friendly with a young doctor. I thought I'd found someone. I was in love—I thought—the way a lonely, damaged girl can fall in love. He was everything to me. But I wouldn't…wouldn't let him make love to me because I didn't know what he'd think. But he kept on at me and eventually I showed him my scarring, even though I was very ashamed of it. He said it was very interesting. Then, a couple of days later, I heard him talking to his friends—the way men do—about me. He said I was a mess, but he could always shut his eyes. He saw me then, and tried to tell me it was just a lad's joke, it didn't matter. But it mattered to me. And when I refused to go out with him again he used to laugh at me, call me the queen of the scars. I got out of there as quickly as I could, and I decided that no man would ever laugh at me again.'

Jonathan didn't comment, even though he could see the tears streaming down her face. 'What would you have done if the operation hadn't worked? If I'd stayed blind, Tania?'

'I would have stayed with you,' she cried. 'You know that! Can't you guess what torture it was for me—hoping you'd see again but knowing that if you did, I'd have to leave you?'

'Would you have married a blind man? If he'd asked you?'

'Of course I would. If I loved him.'

'So you loved me enough perhaps to marry me. But not enough to trust me with your tiny little secret?'

'It's not a tiny little secret to me,' she said.

He stood and came over to her. Taking her two hands, he lifted her from her chair. She was helpless as he held her, kissed her softly on the lips, then pulled her to him. She didn't know how long they stayed there—only that when he tried to move her, her muscles seemed powerless. With his arms round her waist he half carried her to the open caravan door. 'What are you doing?' she asked.

'I'm kissing you. I love kissing you. I just want to kiss you in private.'

The table at the end of the caravan folded down to make a double bed. It was a double bed now—she hadn't bothered to make it this morning. He sat her on it, sat next to her and kissed her some more.

She was wearing a cotton dress that buttoned down the front. It seemed quite proper that after he had finished kissing her neck he should open the top two buttons and kiss the swell of her breasts. He eased her backwards, somehow undoing her bra at the same time. And then his lips were everywhere. Everywhere!

'No, Jonathan,' she cried, and jerked upright. 'I know what you're doing and I don't want you to!'

He didn't try to stop her. 'I was trying to kiss your scars,' he said. 'Now let me.'

'But they're hideous, they're so ugly, you'll go off me and—'

'A girl I know once said that true beauty was in the spirit,' he reminded her. 'I didn't think so then but I do now. I think you're truly beautiful. Now, let me take off your dress.'

For a moment she sat there, her arms crossed protectively over her breasts. Then she stood in front of him, lifted her arms. He took the hem of the dress and drew it over her head.

Her unfastened bra tumbled to the floor. He threw the dress onto the bed. She was standing there in a tiny pair of white bikini pants. And there was her scarring.

He placed his hands on her hips, bent his head and

kissed the angry red weals. The touch of his tongue there—it felt pleasant but it was comforting, too. He eased her back onto the bed, kissed her body time and time again.

'Tania,' he said, 'you are beautiful. Not just beautiful to me, but beautiful to all. And I love you sighted as much as I did when I was blind. You know that?'

'I know it now, Jonathan.' She frowned. 'I'm so sorry I ran away and left you. Why couldn't I have trusted you? It seems so silly now.' She blinked. 'What are you looking for?' He had thrown his jacket to one side. Now he reached for it and was rummaging in the inside pocket.

'I told you, I've been looking for you for two days now. I stayed the night in Buxton and this morning I saw this antique shop—so I went in. I bought myself something to bring me luck.'

She grew wide-eyed as he took out a box and opened it to reveal a ring—a gold ring set with a cabochon-cut emerald surrounded by tiny diamonds.

'It brought me luck,' he said softly, and reached for her hand. 'I love you, Tania. Will you marry me?'

Now years of doubt, troubles, worries were finally settled. Tania could see the love in Jonathan's eyes. He didn't care about her scars! 'Of course I'll marry you,' she breathed. 'Oh, Jonathan, you make me so happy!'

Modern Romance™
...seduction and
passion guaranteed

Tender Romance™
...love affairs that
last a lifetime

Sensual Romance™
...sassy, sexy and
seductive

Blaze
...sultry days and
steamy nights

Medical Romance™
...medical drama on
the pulse

Historical Romance™
...rich, vivid and
passionate

MILLS & BOON®

Winner at

2001 **IDEA** INTERNATIONAL
DESIGN
EFFECTIVENESS
AWARDS

MAT5

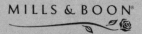

MILLS & BOON®

Medical Romance™

A VERY SINGLE WOMAN by *Caroline Anderson*

Dr Nick Lancaster didn't understand why a beautiful, talented doctor like Helen Moore would want to come to remote Suffolk to work part-time and adopt and raise a child as her own. He had to find out why she'd mothballed her emotions – because she'd blasted all his into the open and raised his masculine instincts for the first time in years!

THE STRANGER'S SECRET by *Maggie Kingsley*

When Greensay Island's only doctor, Jess Arden, broke her leg, she wanted to go on practising but knew she couldn't manage. Then the island's recluse, Ezra Dunbar, revealed himself to be a doctor. Why hadn't he been using his medical skills? And, until he confided his secrets, should Jess be dreaming of their future together?

HER PARTNER'S PASSION by *Carol Wood*

When Dr Abbie Scott returns home from America she discovers a sexy stranger in her home. Whether she likes it or not, Dr Caspar Darke is her new partner and he's here to stay! And living and working together, day and night, makes her aware of how dangerously irresistible he is...

On sale 7th June 2002

0502/03a

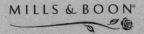

Medical Romance™

THE OUTBACK MATCH *by Lucy Clark*

To the people of Heartfield Dr Halley Ryan is the enemy – sent to close their hospital. And even if they can be won over by her natural friendliness, Dr Max Pearson will not let his feelings towards her be more than professional. He has a secure future mapped out with his fiancée… so why does his heart tell him he's engaged to the wrong woman?

THE PLAYBOY DOCTOR *by Sarah Morgan*

Hardworking and dedicated, Dr Joanna Weston was everything she believed her new locum Seb Macaulay wasn't. Every woman he met adored him and Joanna was determined to be the exception. Little by little Seb's warmth broke down her protective barriers and she began to fall in love with him. But he could so easily break her heart…

CHALLENGING DR BLAKE *by Rebecca Lang*

Working on dangerous assignments had taught World Aid nurse Signy Clover never to develop emotional bonds with anybody. Meeting Dr Dan Blake in the wilderness of Western Canada nearly changed her mind, but she fought their mutual attraction at every step. Winning Signy's love would be the biggest challenge of Dan's life!

On sale 7th June 2002

Available at most branches of WH Smith, Tesco, Martins, Borders, Eason, Sainsbury's and most good paperback bookshops.

0502/03b

2 Books
and a surprise gift!

We would like to take this opportunity to thank you for reading this Mills & Boon® book by offering you the chance to take TWO more specially selected titles from the Medical Romance™ series absolutely FREE! We're also making this offer to introduce you to the benefits of the Reader Service™—

- ★ FREE home delivery
- ★ FREE gifts and competitions
- ★ FREE monthly Newsletter
- ★ Books available before they're in the shops
- ★ Exclusive Reader Service discount

Accepting these FREE books and gift places you under no obligation to buy; you may cancel at any time, even after receiving your free shipment. Simply complete your details below and return the entire page to the address below. **You don't even need a stamp!**

YES! Please send me 2 free Medical Romance books and a surprise gift. I understand that unless you hear from me, I will receive 4 superb new titles every month for just £2.55 each, postage and packing free. I am under no obligation to purchase any books and may cancel my subscription at any time. The free books and gift will be mine to keep in any case.

M2ZEB

Ms/Mrs/Miss/Mr ....Initials ....
BLOCK CAPITALS PLEASE

Surname ....

Address..

....

....Postcode ....

Send this whole page to:
UK: The Reader Service, FREEPOST CN81, Croydon, CR9 3WZ
EIRE: The Reader Service, PO Box 4546, Kilcock, County Kildare (stamp required)